P9-EMC-756

fic
KEE   KEENE, CAROLYN   6775

                    DANA GIRLS MYSTERY

MYSTERY OF THE WAX QUEEN

Blairsville Junior High School
Blairsville, Pennsylvania

MYSTERY OF THE WAX QUEEN

Louise and Jean Dana are thrilled when their uncle asks them to solve a very puzzling and fascinating mystery involving two Wax Queens, one of them alive!

Their detective work takes the Danas to a quaint Greenwich Village shop in New York City. Here they meet and are baffled by a sculptress with extra-sensory perception. Weird adventures confront Louise and Jean as they attempt to unravel the mystery of a valuable wax bust of Queen Victoria which suddenly and strangely appears in the sculptress' shop, then disappears. Two young women who frequently change disguises and a man suspected of operating a car-winning racket try hard to scare Louise and Jean off the case.

How the teen-age sleuths, with the help of their friends Ken Scott and Chris Barton, find the solution to this tantalizing mystery is revealed in the breath-taking climax.

"Look!" Jean exclaimed. "A diamond."

The *Dana Girls* Mystery Stories

MYSTERY
of the
WAX QUEEN

By Carolyn Keene

GROSSET & DUNLAP
A National General Company
Publishers   *New York*

© 1966, 1972 BY GROSSET & DUNLAP, INC.
ALL RIGHTS RESERVED
PUBLISHED SIMULTANEOUSLY IN CANADA
LIBRARY OF CONGRESS CATALOG CARD NUMBER: 78–180993
ISBN: 0–448–09084–8

PRINTED IN THE UNITED STATES OF AMERICA

CONTENTS

MYSTERY
OF THE
WAX QUEEN

CHAPTER I

Crashing Canvas

"I CAN'T stand the suspense!" exclaimed Jean Dana. Her blue eyes swept over her three companions. "How can you be so calm?"

She was standing with her sister Louise and two school friends in a crowded carnival tent. Before them on a bunting-draped platform was a sleek red sports car.

"Who's calm?" said Louise. "If you had my butterflies!" She was seventeen, a year older than her sister, and had soft brown hair.

"I'd die if I won it," Doris Harland said breathlessly. "How much longer before the drawing, Evelyn?"

Dark-haired Evelyn Starr looked at her watch. "Two minutes." Her wistful face brightened. "I just know I'm going to win!"

Suddenly, through the excited buzz of voices,

the four friends heard a man's hoarse whisper: "Crying won't help! I'm warning you, get out and stay out! If you don't—" The threat remained unfinished.

The Danas and their friends looked around to see who had spoken, but there were no men near them. The girls were standing close to a screen which extended from the front edge of the platform, providing a small backstage area at one side.

"The voice must have come from behind there," Jean said softly.

As she spoke, a spattering of applause and cheers broke out in the tent and a slender, shrewd-looking man strode onto the stage, smiling and waving.

"And now, ladies and gentlemen, time for the big event!" His eyes appraised the audience carefully.

"Third, second, first—that's how we'll draw the prizes!" The man's brassy voice filled the tent. Was he the one who had whispered the threat?

The next moment he pointed at Louise. "Will the pretty brunette step up and pick a number from the barrel?"

Blushing, Louise went up the few steps to the platform. The crowd waited breathlessly as she reached into a large brown barrel and drew out a ticket. The announcer glanced at it, then called out, "Number 32!" A young man hurried forward to claim third prize—a record player.

Louise stepped down and an elderly man was chosen to draw the ticket for second prize, which turned out to be a television set.

"Now—" said the announcer. He paused and an excited stir ran through the audience. Then he flashed a gleaming smile. "—for first prize!" Who is going to win this great big gorgeous sports car?"

"Oh, I am—please!" breathed Jean.

The man squared his shoulders and again looked over the audience. Finally he smiled at a pretty girl with blond hair, which she wore piled high. "I know you will pick the winning number for just the right person."

Wearing a smartly tailored pink coat, she sauntered gracefully to the stage.

"Mix up the numbers," the man instructed her, "and pick the lucky one."

The audience watched tensely as the girl put her hand in the barrel and stirred the tickets. She was about to withdraw one when the announcer said, "Wait!" He assumed a nonchalant look and said, "Did I ever tell you folks about the time my brother chased a greased pig into the china shop?" The crowd groaned and laughed as the showman teased them, pretending he was going to tell a long story.

Suddenly he stepped forward and said in a stage whisper, "Now you know I wouldn't make you wait any longer!"

As the audience laughed, the Danas and their

friends exchanged quick looks. That was the voice they had heard behind the screen!

"Take out the ticket!" boomed the announcer.

But before the girl could do so, a woman's piercing voice rang out: "Stop him! Stop him!"

Everyone stared at the middle-aged figure pushing her way toward the platform. Her light hair was disheveled and there was a wild look in her eyes.

Pointing frantically to the announcer, she exclaimed, "Make him stop!"

A policeman quickly made his way from one side of the tent and seized the woman's arm. "Come with me," he ordered. She gasped in surprise, and her cheeks reddened. Looking confused, she allowed herself to be escorted from the tent.

As the audience broke into excited chatter, Doris asked the other girls, "What was that all about?"

"Search me," Jean replied. "Maybe there's something crooked about this whole deal."

Doris laughed. "That's the detective speaking now!"

The announcer quieted the curious audience. "I'm sorry for that interruption. Are you ready to go on with the drawing?"

"Oh, hurry up!" shouted one of the spectators.

The girl smiled. "All right. Here goes!"

She handed a number to the announcer, who shouted, "Who has Number 1196? Will the lucky

"Stop him!" the woman cried out

owner of this beautiful car please come forward?"

Jean crumpled her ticket. "It's none of us," she said with a sigh.

For a couple of seconds there was silence, then a red-haired girl near the back of the tent held up a ticket. "I— Oh, I can't believe it!"

The pale-faced girl, who was about twenty years old, made her way to the platform to present her stub. The onlookers clapped wildly and murmured how lucky she was.

News photographers began to take flashbulb pictures. Reporters, with notebooks and pencils in hand, busily scribbled down her name and address. "Dolores Doremus," she said, trying to catch her breath. "I live in Amesboro."

The announcer told her that the car had been provided with dealer's license plates and reminded her to register the car in her name within twenty-four hours.

"The car's all set to go. Congratulations and safe driving, Miss Doremus!"

"Thank you so much," she said. "That is very kind."

As the Danas and their friends turned to leave, Doris sighed and patted her blond hair into place. "I was going to give you all a ride back to school tonight in my beautiful red car, but I guess we'll have to go in the Starhurst station wagon."

The girls laughed. As they walked out of the tent, they discussed the strange woman. "Why did she want to stop the drawing?" Evelyn asked.

"I think she's probably sick," Doris remarked.

"I'll bet she was the one we heard the announcer threatening," said Jean.

Louise had been listening thoughtfully. "Here comes Mr. Hovis, the chairman," she said. "Let's ask him about the man."

"Hello, girls," the chairman greeted them. "Well, what did you think of the carnival?"

Jean spoke first. "It was simply marvelous. We didn't miss a thing—Ferris wheel, merry-go-round, all the target games—everything!"

"And I'm so full of ice cream and candy apples I could burst!" Doris laughed.

"I think we made a lot of money for the Penfield Hospital," said Mr. Hovis.

"That's wonderful," Louise responded, then asked hesitantly, "By the way, Mr. Hovis, who was the announcer at the car raffle and how did he become connected with the carnival?"

"His name is Denver," the chairman replied. "He took complete charge of the whole event. Supplied all the prizes donated by local shops and distributed the ticket books."

"Did he turn in all the money?" Jean quickly asked.

Mr. Hovis laughed. "Yes, of course, but he only handled a few of the books. The others were sold by the committee."

Still suspicious, Jean questioned, "Perhaps one

of the books Mr. Denver sold contained the car-winning ticket?"

"I have no idea. There were so many tickets—" The chairman dropped his voice and scrutinized the girl's serious face. "You have doubts about him, haven't you?"

Jean brushed a few strands of hair from her forehead. "I'm wondering how that woman who tried to interfere with the drawing fits in."

"Too bad, wasn't it?" the chairman said. "The officer escorted her off the grounds. He told me afterward that Mr. Denver said the woman was an unbalanced relative of his, who has been making trouble for him lately. Denver asked the policeman to intercept her if she showed up."

Mr. Hovis smiled. "So far as the carnival is concerned, everything was on the up and up. Glad you enjoyed it." He quickly excused himself and hurried off.

As the girls walked toward the exit from the carnival grounds, the wind whipped their skirts and hair. Above the bright lights, the sky was black. "Storm's coming up," said Louise.

Tents and booths were already being taken down. "Here's one that's still open," Evelyn remarked. "How about a snack?"

"Good idea!" Louise grinned. "A hamburger and a glass of milk would be great!"

"Not me, thank you," said Doris. "I'll just watch."

There were almost a dozen customers milling about the stand in the tent. The three hungry girls were served in a few minutes and stood at the counter munching hamburgers.

A rumble of thunder sounded, and the wind rose and buffeted the tent. Suddenly there was a loud ripping noise and one side flapped loose, torn by the wind. The canvas billowed, straining at the ropes.

"Look!" Jean screamed. The tall center pole was swaying!

An instant later it crashed down, burying everyone under the canvas!

CHAPTER II

Mystery Offer

"HELP!" a woman screamed and there were cries of "Get me out of here!" The falling canvas had short-circuited the lights and darkness added to the confusion.

Louise was lying face down on the ground. Humping her back, she managed to push up the heavy weight of the canvas and call to her sister and friends. Amid the groans and shouts around her, she heard no answer from them.

"I must get out," she thought. "Then I can help the others!"

She inched her way over the ground toward one edge of the fallen tent and finally reached fresh air, where she stood up shakily. By this time, rescuers had come running and were lifting up the ends of the canvas.

Flashlights were beamed under it and Louise saw people struggling to get up, while others lay still. She bent low and hurried underneath to where she saw Doris and Evelyn scrambling to their knees.

"You all right?" Louise scanned their faces.

"I—I guess so," Evelyn replied shakily.

"Sure," said Doris. "Where's Jean?"

The girls looked around quickly. "There!" exclaimed Louise. Her sister lay unmoving beside the wreckage of the refreshment stand.

Anxiously Louise hurried over and knelt beside Jean. She felt her pulse. "It's kind of weak," she said to the other two girls, "but she only fainted."

"Need some help?" asked a masculine voice.

One of the rescuers had paused beside the girls. Louise asked him to carry Jean outside, where he put her down on the grass.

Jean's eyelids fluttered.

"Shall I get a doctor?" he asked.

"She's coming around now," said Doris.

"We'll call if we need one," Louise said, and thanked the man as he hurried away to assist the rescuers.

Jean's eyes opened. "Where am I?" she asked. "What happened?" Then she grinned weakly. "I remember hitting my head on the refreshment stand."

"Are you okay?" Louise asked anxiously.

Jean sat up and rubbed her head. "I've got a small lump there, but I guess I'll live."

With a rueful grin, she got up. "Maybe we ought to help the others," Jean remarked.

But as she glanced at the scene of the accident, she saw that the rescue operation was well in hand, though hampered by the strong winds that had caused the tent to collapse.

The storm, which had been rising, now broke in a torrent of rain.

"Oh!" exclaimed Jean. "The end of a perfect evening!"

"We'd better get back to school," Louise said. "News of the accident may have been on the radio. If Mrs. Crandall heard it, she'll be worried."

Mrs. Crandall was headmistress of Starhurst. Though stern, she was always fair in her judgments and the Danas liked her very much.

Evelyn began to laugh. "Wait till she sees us!" The girls looked at one another and broke into laughter. The front of Louise's pink suit was brown with dust, which was rapidly turning to mud under the rain. Jean's trim navy coat had a torn hem—and like the other two girls, the Danas had dirt-streaked faces.

"Oh," gasped Doris, "we're a mess!"

"It isn't funny," said Jean, trying to keep a straight face. "Our clothes are ruined!" She broke into giggles again.

"Come on," said Louise. "It won't help to stand here getting soaked."

"It can't make us look any worse," said Evelyn as she followed the others, still laughing.

By the time the girls reached the main exit, they were drenched. As they made their way through the crowd on the sidewalk, the Starhurst station wagon pulled up to the curb.

When the school driver saw them, he stared, speechless.

"We're all right, really," Louise reassured him. The girls told him what had happened.

"We've just been a little hysterical," Evelyn added and sighed, exhausted.

The driver shook his head. "You're lucky you weren't hurt bad."

He drove carefully through the downpour toward the main part of Penfield. They had just passed through it and gone a short distance, when there came a sudden loud honking from behind them. The school driver pulled far to the right.

A moment later a car shot past them with two girls in it.

"There goes that red car—the first prize!" Jean exclaimed.

"Yes, I see the dealer's plates," Louise said as the station wagon's headlights illuminated the back of the speeding car.

"And look!" Doris cried out. Following the red car was a black sedan.

"That's Mr. Denver, I think!" Louise exclaimed.

"It is!" Jean said excitedly. "I got a good look at him!"

The red car speeded up, and the black one did the same.

"What's the idea? Is he chasing those girls?" Evelyn asked.

Jean leaned forward toward the driver's shoulder. "Follow those cars!" she urged. "Please!"

The school driver shook his head. "That would be against the rules, miss. If those folks are having any trouble, it's best not to get mixed up in it."

Though the girls realized he was right, their curiosity had been piqued. It was not long before both speeding cars were out of sight.

Doris chuckled. "I was just remembering that Mr. Denver wished the winner safe driving."

Louise and Jean looked at each other. They were sure there was some mystery connected with what they had just seen. The Danas' friends often said the two sisters had an instinct for mysteries. Recently at Starhurst School they had solved *The Riddle of the Frozen Fountain* and when on vacation in Florida uncovered *The Secret of the Silver Dolphin.*

When the station wagon parked in front of the main building of the school, the night watchman opened the door for the girls.

He stared in amazement at their rumpled appearance, but before he could say anything,

Louise asked, "Is Mrs. Crandall worried about us?"

"No, Miss Dana," the man replied. "Everything has been quiet here. Whatever happened?"

Briefly the girls told him, then started for their rooms.

"Wait!" he said. "You surprised me so that I forgot to give you a message!"

"Oh, what was it?" asked Jean.

"A man in New York City has been trying to get you girls on the phone all evening." He handed Louise a piece of paper. "He finally left word you were to call this number the instant you came back." The number was unfamiliar to both sisters.

"Didn't the man leave his name?" Jean asked.

The watchman frowned. "Well, yes, he did, but there was static on the line and I didn't quite catch it. He said the call was urgent, though."

Mystified, Louise and Jean went to a telephone booth at the far end of the corridor and Louise called the number. The receiver was picked up instantly and a deep voice boomed, "Hello!"

Louise started to ask who it was, then broke off and beamed with joy. "Uncle Ned! You're in port!"

Captain Dana was master of the *Balaska*, a transatlantic liner.

"My ship's in dock for repairs," he said, "and

I'm staying with Cousin Cynthia. Now then," he added, "are you ready for a big surprise, my hearties?"

"Yes," said Louise. "Tell us!"

"Tell us what?" whispered Jean. "I'm dying of curiosity."

Louise shared the receiver with her sister and both girls' eyes sparkled at their uncle's next words.

"How'd you like to solve a mystery in New York?"

"Would we!" they chorused. As their questions tumbled out, Captain Dana exclaimed:

"Hold hard there! One at a time!" Then he chuckled. "All I know is it's a weird one, but I'll leave the telling to Cynthia. It's her mystery." He explained that the girls' cousin was hoping they would come to New York to spend their spring vacation with her.

"Sounds marvelous," said Louise. "But what about Aunt Harriet? She'll be looking for us at home."

Orphaned at an early age, Louise and Jean lived with their bachelor uncle and maiden aunt, who were brother and sister. The girls loved the salty sea captain and sweet, understanding aunt as if they had been their own father and mother.

"Now don't you worry about that," Captain Dana said. "Harriet is invited down here too. I suppose," he went on, "you girls are in the middle of exams. Well, I wish you all the luck in the world."

"We'll need it!" Jean called into the phone.

"Please, Uncle Ned," Louise begged, "give us just one little hint about the mystery."

The captain laughed. "All right," he said. "Did you ever hear of the Wax Queen?"

For a moment the girls were too surprised to say anything. "Wax Queen?" Louise exclaimed. "Who is she?"

Jean giggled. "Is she made of wax?"

"One is, one isn't," her uncle replied with a chuckle. "There are two of 'em. You can take your choice!"

"What do you mean?" Louise asked, puzzled.

"And what is weird about it?" Jean put in.

"Well," said the captain uncomfortably, "I don't like spooky business—hearing voices and all that." Then he said crisply, "Never mind. Cynthia will tell you." He refused to answer any more questions, but told them that their aunt would arrive in New York about the same time they would.

"That'll be Saturday morning," he said. "I went ahead and made reservations for you," he added with a chuckle. "You can pick up the tickets at your airport." He said good night and the girls hung up.

"Uncle Ned certainly made that mystery clear as mud," Jean said with a smile.

"It sounds fascinating," Louise remarked. "I just can't wait!"

The girls hurried upstairs to their two-room suite, consisting of a study and a bedroom. Getting ready for bed, they discussed the upcoming exams.

"We'll really have to hit the books," said Jean, then she grinned. "If the going gets too tough, we can always think about our Friday night date at Walton Academy. Chris Barton sure is a cool dancer."

Louise laughed. "Ken Scott is just as cool."

All the next day the girls studied quietly. After dinner they went back to their books, leaving the door to their suite ajar. Concentrating deeply, they were not aware of someone peering in from the hall.

Suddenly the quiet was broken by a small *bang!*

The girls jumped. "What was that?" Jean asked.

There was no need for Louise to answer. A sickening odor was filling the room.

CHAPTER III

The Strange Letter

"UGH! Let's get out of here!" Jean urged.

Holding their breath, Louise and Jean ran into the corridor. Several students with rooms nearby, having heard the explosion, rushed out to see what had happened.

"Oh, what a dreadful smell!" cried one of the freshmen. She was a small, pretty girl named Ruth Bolen. "Where did it come from?"

Louise raised her eyebrows in disgust. "A skunk bomb. It's just inside our door."

"*Eek!*" said Ruth. She retreated into her own room and closed the door.

The Danas hurried back into their suite and opened every window. Then Jean scooped the remains of the skunk bomb into an envelope, and they returned to the hall, shutting the door behind them.

By this time Doris and Evelyn had come up. "What happened?" Doris asked.

When she was told, her eyes wandered down the corridor to a room shared by Lettie Briggs and Ina Mason. Doris whispered, "I'll bet Lettie's guilty!"

Everyone knew that Lettie disliked the Danas. She envied their reputation as amateur detectives and often played tricks on the sisters, trying to discredit them.

"It's strange," said Jean, "that neither Lettie nor Ina came out to see what the commotion was."

"Let's try to find some proof," Louise suggested.

Both sisters searched the hall between their room and Lettie's. Suddenly Louise spotted a red silk tassel on the floor. Triumphantly she held it up. "We all know this is from Lettie's bathrobe!" she said.

Evelyn spoke up. "And it wasn't there when we went to our rooms, because I'd have seen it. I lost my fountain pen and looked along here for it."

There was no chance for further conversation, for at that moment Mrs. Crandall came marching down the corridor from the front stairway. The headmistress, a tall, severe-looking woman, had learned of the bomb incident, and demanded to know the details.

"We're not sure of anything except that someone threw it into our study," Jean answered.

Frowning, Mrs. Crandall strode to the suite,

looked inside, then quickly shut the door again. "I assume you were studying for your exams tomorrow," she said to the Danas. "You had better take your books into someone else's room until your suite is completely aired."

Jean gave Mrs. Crandall the envelope with the fragments of the bomb in it, which the headmistress said she would dispose of outside the building.

While Mrs. Crandall had been questioning Louise and Jean, the students who had gathered in the hall returned to their rooms. Ruth Bolen peered out and beckoned the sisters to come in.

"I just remembered something," Ruth said. "I don't like to tell tales, but I did overhear Lettie say to Ina, 'The Danas make me sick with their good marks. I'll fix them so they won't be able to study.' I've been so worried about the math exam," she added seriously, "that I forgot all about it."

Louise and Jean nodded at each other. This and the bathrobe tassel were good proof! They thanked Ruth and went back to their suite to gather books, papers, and pencils which they took into Evelyn's room.

"Are you going to give the tassel back to Lettie and accuse her of throwing the skunk bomb?" Evelyn asked.

Louise shook her head. "One good turn deserves another," she said, grinning mischievously.

Organizing her work on the far side of Evelyn's desk, Jean said, "What should we do about Lettie?"

Louise's eyes twinkled. "You remember when we got Lettie a date with three little boys and she thought a big handsome man was coming? How about a similar trick, only this time no one will show up?"

Jean giggled. "Perfect."

Louise took a plain piece of paper and printed a note to Lettie in bold letters, then signed it Jack Brownley. "Does it look mannish?" she asked the others.

Evelyn giggled. "Yes. Who's Jack Brownley?"

"Nobody. I made him up."

"Do you suppose Lettie will fall for it?" Evelyn asked.

"Of course," said Jean. "She'll think he's some secret admirer."

"If I mail this now," Louise said, "it should be picked up at eleven o'clock and delivered to-morrow."

She hurried out, taking the invitation and the tassel. After the note was mailed, she slipped into the dining room and placed the silk tassel beside Lettie's plate.

Then the girls settled down to study. At ten o'clock they were finished and returned to their room. The odor gone, Louise and Jean slept soundly.

At breakfast time, when they reached the dining room, Lettie had already pocketed the tassel. When Louise and Jean walked past her, she did not even look up to say good morning. During the day, Lettie was forgotten as the Danas concentrated on their exams. Even the mystery of the Wax Queen did not enter their thoughts until they were dressing for dinner. Who was the Queen? And what was so mysterious about her?

"It'll be fun sleuthing in New York," said Louise.

There was a knock on their study door. Jean opened it. One of the underclassmen handed her a special-delivery letter. "This just came," she said.

The envelope bore no return address and had been mailed in Penfield. The handwriting was unfamiliar.

Tearing open the letter addressed to her and Louise, Jean read the short note aloud:

" 'Dear Misses Dana,

I have heard you are good amateur sleuths. It is important that I locate Mr. Denver, the man in charge of the carnival prizes. Please, if you know where he is or can find out for me, I will be eternally grateful. Address a letter to General Delivery, New York, N. Y.

Sincerely,
Winifred Moffat' "

"How strange!" Louise commented. "Jean, did you ever hear of Winifred Moffat?"

"No." Jean paused. "Could this be another one of Lettie's jokes?"

"I doubt it." Louise shook her head. "She wouldn't know about Mr. Denver."

The girls recalled their suspicions of Denver. "Do you think Winifred Moffat could be the woman who tried to stop the drawing of the prizes?" Jean asked.

"I've a hunch she was," Louise replied.

The dinner bell rang and the sisters joined their friends on the way to the dining room. Lettie was particularly dressed up and had a bright smile on her face. Louise and Jean were sure she was eagerly awaiting her date that evening.

During the social hour after dinner, the Danas, together with Doris and Evelyn, made a point of watching Lettie. As time went on, her cheerful face became gloomy. The girls overheard Ina say, "Don't be blue, Lettie. I'm sure he'll be here any minute."

But Ina's prediction did not come true. When the gong sounded for study hour, Lettie, crestfallen, dawdled back to her room.

"You know what?" Louise said as the Danas started for their suite. "I'm sorry I played that joke. Now she *is* upset and probably won't be able to study. But I think we can make it up to her."

"How?" asked Jean.

Louise offered to call Ken Scott at Walton Academy and see if he could fix Lettie up with a blind date for the dance the next evening.

Jean nodded. "Ken will understand. He'll pick some nice boy just right for Lettie. And if he has a big family name, it'll be all the better. Lettie loves to feel important."

When Ken heard the request, he remarked, "I know just the one. Leave it to me. I'll have him call Lettie in a few minutes."

The next day Lettie announced smugly that she had a date with John Case, whose father was a very important judge. The Danas congratulated her and smiled to themselves.

At four o'clock the last exam was over and Starhurst's corridors rang with whoops of joy and excited chatter.

That evening the school bus transported some of the girls to Walton Academy. Their dates greeted them with broad smiles and lovely corsages. Louise's friend, Ken Scott, was tall, blond, and athletic. Jean's date was Chris Barton, a dark-haired boy with laughing eyes. He was full of fun and always won the comic roles in school plays. Winking at the sisters, Ken and Chris pointed to another couple.

A lanky boy with horn-rimmed glasses was introducing himself to Lettie. "You are Miss Briggs?"

Lettie snickered. "Yes, I am. Oh, how did you

hear about me? It was simply marvelous of you to invite me." Quickly slipping her arm through his, she accompanied the spindle-legged boy inside.

When the dance was over, the girls thanked Ken and Chris for a wonderful time and invited them to visit Starhurst a month later.

As the girls boarded the school bus, Chris grinned broadly. "Don't be surprised if we turn up in New York City while you're there," he said.

"That would be great," Jean replied.

In the morning the Danas took an early flight out of Penfield Airport. Before long, the sleek silver plane was setting down at LaGuardia Airport. At the exit gate Aunt Harriet and Uncle Ned were eagerly waiting for their nieces.

"It's so good to see you, my dears," said Miss Dana, hugging them tightly. The girls complimented her on her attractive suit and perky hat.

"My new spring outfit," she told them.

Uncle Ned was a tall, broad-shouldered man with a commanding air and a twinkle in his eyes. "Glad you made it," he said, kissing Louise first, then Jean. "How was the trip, my hearties?"

"Just great. We're so happy to see you again," Louise said.

Jean added, "And we just can't wait to hear all about the Wax Queen."

The Danas took a taxi to Cynthia Carson's apartment building, an old-fashioned, elegant one with a pleasant doorman. Uncle Ned led them to the self-service elevator and pushed the button for the fifth floor. "Cynthia has Apartment 53," the captain told them.

Louise and Jean had not seen their cousin for several years, but found she had changed very little. She was a lively, congenial widow of fifty.

"I am so thrilled you could come," she said. "Let me show you to your rooms first and then we'll have lunch. You girls must be hungry after your trip."

Jean laughed. "How did you guess?"

A few minutes later she and Louise joined Mrs. Carson in the cheerfully decorated kitchen. It had been modernized somewhat, but like many old-fashioned apartments had a fire escape outside one of the windows.

The girls helped carry the delicious meal of chicken in a casserole, potato puffs, and tossed salad into the dining room.

When everyone was seated and served, Jean said, "Please, Cousin Cynthia, tell us all about the Wax Queen."

Mrs. Carson smiled. "Actually there are two of them—both mysterious. One is a real woman. The other is a very old wax bust of Queen Victoria. It is a priceless piece."

"And it has disappeared!" put in Jean impetuously.

"Just the opposite," replied her cousin. "It has suddenly and mysteriously *appeared* in a shop downtown. I will take you girls there tomorrow."

"Tell us more," Louise begged.

"Later," her cousin said firmly. "Then we can talk it over quietly. Now I want to catch up on all the news."

When lunch was over, Mrs. Carson said, "I have planned something for this afternoon and I hope you don't mind. A friend sold me several chances on a new car. The drawing is being held at a bazaar in a New Jersey hotel and I thought you would enjoy the trip."

Car! Bazaar! Lucky-number drawing! Would Mr. Denver be in charge? Louise and Jean were excited at the prospect. Maybe they could find out more about the mysterious man.

While the sisters helped clear the table and tidy the kitchen, Aunt Harriet decided to mail a letter and make a purchase in a nearby drugstore. Fifteen minutes later, as the others were gathering in the living room, there came a loud scream from just outside the door.

"Help!" a woman's voice cried.

Louise jumped from her chair. "That's Aunt Harriet!" she exclaimed.

CHAPTER IV

Winners and Wigs

LOUISE flung open the door to the hall. Miss Dana was lying on the floor in front of the apartment.

"Aunt Harriet! What happened?" cried Louise as the sisters hurried to help her up.

"That man!" Miss Dana gasped, pointing toward the elevator. "He took my purse and knocked me down!"

The girls looked up to see a burly man with a dark beard and mustache boarding the elevator. An instant later the door shut and he was borne downward.

Louise, Jean, and Uncle Ned dashed to the stairway alongside the elevator. The girls, more agile than the captain, reached the first floor ahead of him.

"That man who just came down—where did he go?" Jean quickly asked the doorman.

"You mean the bearded one who asked for Mrs. Carson?"

"He's a thief!" Jean cried impatiently. "Did he come out this way?"

The doorman looked confused. "He went out the front, but I didn't notice which way he walked."

The girls rushed to the street and looked up and down, but did not see the purse snatcher.

"He could have jumped into a passing taxi," said Louise, "or ducked down into the subway at the next corner. We'd never find him there."

Disappointed, the girls returned to the apartment house. Uncle Ned was questioning the doorman. The attendant apologized for letting the thief in. "He looked all right to me. He showed a calling card. I couldn't read it because I don't have my glasses with me, but I didn't want to tell him that. I guess I should have checked with Mrs. Carson on the house phone."

The Danas said nothing to reproach him. As they entered the elevator they saw Aunt Harriet's open purse on the floor. Louise picked it up. *There was nothing inside!*

"Poor Aunt Harriet!" said Jean as they rode up to the fifth floor. "I wonder how much money was taken."

When they reached the apartment, Cousin Cynthia asked hopefully, "Did you catch him?"

"No," Louise replied, "but we found this in the elevator." She gave the purse to her aunt.

Captain Dana asked his sister how much money she had been carrying.

"About a hundred dollars in traveler's checks," she replied, "and a hundred in cash."

The others expressed their sympathy, knowing there was little hope of recovering the cash.

Aunt Harriet said, "I can't understand why that man took everything—even my lipstick and powder."

"Because he was in a big hurry," Jean said. "He probably jammed everything into his pockets, expecting to sort out the valuables later."

Cousin Cynthia looked worried. "Harriet, you took a key to this apartment. Did you put it in your bag?"

Miss Dana gasped. "Oh dear, I did! The thief might come back here to rob us."

"Well, this is a fine how-do-you-do," said Captain Dana, frowning. "Guess I'm elected to be your official bodyguard."

Mrs. Carson smiled. "You needn't bother, Ned. See that bookcase over there, full of books? We can move it in front of the door."

"But then how will we get in and out of the apartment?" Jean asked.

"Through my hidden door to the hall," Cousin Cynthia answered. "Come, I'll show you."

She led the way to the kitchen and drew aside a curtain which the girls had assumed hid pots and pans. Behind it was a door.

"I have several keys to this," she assured the Danas, and distributed four which had been hidden under some napkins in a drawer.

"I'll report the robbery to the superintendent and ask to have my other door lock changed." After making the call, she said, "The lock will have to wait until Monday. The locksmith who is always used by this building is away for the week-end."

Mrs. Carson then called the police. An officer came to question Miss Dana about the purse-snatching incident. He made notes, including a description of the man, and said the police would get in touch with her if he was picked up.

As soon as the officer had gone, the bookcase was moved against the living-room door, and the Danas left the apartment. The captain had business to attend to on the *Balaska* and Aunt Harriet went to the bank to see about replacing her traveler's checks.

Mrs. Carson and the girls boarded a bus for New Jersey. On the way, the Danas told her about Mr. Denver. An hour later the three entered the Suburban Hotel, where the bazaar was being held. In the gaily decorated ballroom they threaded their way through the crowd to the shiny sports sedan on display near the stage.

"It's a real beauty!" Jean noted.

They looked around but saw no sign of Mr. Denver. Then the girls followed Cynthia Carson to a display table and admired the lovely flower pins arranged on a green felt cloth. After selecting a few for gifts, they went to the main dining room for an early dinner.

"Oh, I hope Mr. Denver will be emcee tonight," Louise said, gazing about the well-lighted room. "If we have the chance, I think we should ask him how he knows Winifred Moffat. It would be interesting to watch his reaction."

"We must observe the drawing closely, too," said Jean, "to see if we can spot anything crooked."

"Let me check if Mr. Denver is emcee," Cousin Cynthia offered. "Here comes the chairman of the bazaar." She stopped the woman as she was sweeping past, and introduced her as Mrs. Bluett.

"Louise and Jean are curious to know who is in charge of the drawing," she said.

"Oh, some professional who does this all the time. His name is Denver."

Louise and Jean were gleeful. They could hardly wait for the drawing to begin.

Time passed slowly until nine o'clock when Mrs. Bluett invited everyone holding tickets to step closer to the stage, where the lucky numbers would be picked.

The Danas and their cousin stood near the car,

which was close to the left stage door. They surmised that Mr. Denver would come out that way,
and hoped to talk with him. A moment later the
slick emcee strode, smiling, from the wings. He
was carrying the large barrel which he had used
for the numbers in Penfield.

His performance followed the same pattern as
the one he had given there. Finally he chose a
girl to draw the ticket for the car.

As she went through the stage door near the
Danas, Jean grabbed Louise's arm. "She looks like
the girl who won the car in Penfield! Only now
her hair isn't red! She's wearing a black wig!"

The sisters watched intently as the pale-faced
girl walked from the wings. She put her hand
into the barrel and stirred the numbers around.
Finally she pulled one out and handed it to Mr.
Denver.

"Number 407 wins!" he announced. "Who has
the matching stub?"

Another young woman in the crowd raised her
hand, then went through the same stage door, and
onto the stage.

It was Louise's turn to nudge Jean. "And she
is the same blond-haired girl who drew the winning
number at the carnival! But now she is wearing a
brown wig!"

"Something's phony about this whole thing,"
Jean declared. "I'm going for a policeman. As soon

as those three come down here, you start a conversation and try to hold them until I get back!"

"Wait," said Louise. "We'd better get a closer look at those girls to be sure we're not mistaken."

"I guess you're right," Jean agreed.

The crowd clapped loudly as Mr. Denver congratulated the winner. Then he and the two young women disappeared into the wings. A full minute went by and no one came out the stage door.

"That's odd," Louise said. "What's happened to them?"

When a few more minutes had passed and the three still had not appeared, Louise told their cousin they were going backstage. "Jean, you go through the far door. I'll go through this one."

To the girls' utter astonishment, there was no one in the wings. At the rear of the left wing was an exit.

"They must have gone out there," Jean said, and hurried to look outside. No one was in sight.

"Why would they have run away without claiming the car?" Louise asked, puzzled.

"Maybe Mrs. Bluett has the answer," Jean suggested.

The girls returned to the large hall and found the chairman chatting with friends.

"Pardon me, Mrs. Bluett," Louise said, "but why didn't the lucky winner claim the car?"

The woman smiled. "Oh, that car on the floor is just a sample lent to us by the motor company. The winner must go directly to the dealer and get one like it."

"Who is the dealer?" Jean asked politely.

"Dear me," said Mrs. Bluett, "I can't remember. You see, Mr. Denver attended to the whole matter and I didn't pay much attention. Why, is something wrong?"

"There may be," said Louise.

Before Mrs. Bluett could question them further, the girls hurried to the hotel lobby and asked the desk clerk if he knew the name of the dealer who had supplied the car for the drawing. He shook his head. "No. I'm sorry. Let me ask our manager." He disappeared into an inner room but came back in a few moments to say the manager did not know, either. "He suggested, however, you try the Acme Motor Sales Company. It's around the corner from here."

The girls reached the white brick building just before closing time. The dealer told them that his company had not supplied the sports car for the bazaar, and he did not know who had. Disappointed, they started back to the hotel.

"There's no telling where Mr. Denver went to pick up the car," Jean said. "By the time we find out, he'll have been there and gone."

"But we might get a lead on him from Mrs.

Bluett," Louise suggested. "Let's try to catch her before she leaves."

They found the woman talking with Cousin Cynthia in the lobby. Louise quickly explained their suspicions. "We don't want to alert the police," she said, "until we're sure he *is* running a racket. Do you know where we could find him?"

Mrs. Bluett was distressed by what the girls had told her, and explained that the man had called her and offered his services. She took a card from her purse. "He gave me this address and phone number, but they belong to an answering service."

Jean hurried off and called the number. In a short time she was back. "Dead end," she reported gloomily. "The service says he is on the road now and no longer lives at the address he gave them when he registered."

"What bad luck!" said Cousin Cynthia, and suggested that they start for home.

When they reached the apartment, Captain Dana was there, reading the evening paper. He reported everything had been quiet. "I guess that thief was too scared to come back. I told the night man to keep a lookout for him. Unless the fellow is disguised, I don't think he'll get in."

"Let's hope not!" said Aunt Harriet, coming from the kitchen where she had prepared a midnight snack.

When Louise had finished her sandwich and milk, she decided to send Winifred Moffat a note, telling where the Danas had seen Mr. Denver that evening. As instructed, she addressed the envelope to General Delivery, New York, N. Y.

Uncle Ned offered to take the letter to a mailbox halfway up the street. "I'd like to get a little fresh air before turning in," he remarked.

The girls said good night and went to their room. They snuggled into the soft beds and soon were sound asleep.

Suddenly the sisters were jolted awake by a tremendous *crash!*

CHAPTER V

The Wax Queen

THE two girls leaped from their beds.

"The bookcase, I'll bet!" exclaimed Jean.

Swiftly they put on slippers, grabbed their robes, and hastened into the dining room, where they turned on the light. Nothing there! Cautiously they went into the dark living room.

Jean flicked the switch. "I knew it!" she said. The bookcase had crashed forward, spilling its entire contents. The hall door stood open and it was evident that someone had tried to push the tall case aside to enter the room.

"Oh, no!" exclaimed Aunt Harriet as she hurried in with Cousin Cynthia. Uncle Ned arrived a moment later from his room at the rear of the hall.

Louise and Jean dashed out of the apartment with their uncle and rang for the elevator. It came up immediately.

As the three rode down to the lobby of the apartment house, Jean remarked, "The indicator showed the elevator came up from the first floor. The intruder may be hiding there."

When they reached the lobby, Captain Dana insisted upon stepping out first. "If that thief is around, I want to tackle him. You girls keep out of it."

But the softly lighted lobby appeared to be empty. Then Louise exclaimed, "Look!" There was a man crumpled on the floor near the front door. They rushed to his side.

"The night doorman!" Jean exclaimed.

"He's unconscious," said Uncle Ned.

As the Danas tried to revive the man, they detected a sharp odor around him.

"I believe something was sprayed here to put him to sleep for a while," said Louise. "I suppose our would-be burglar hoped to ransack the apartment and make his escape before this man came to."

Uncle Ned opened the front door and let in a strong gust of fresh cool air. Within a couple of minutes the doorman revived. They helped him to a chair and then asked him what had happened.

"A stranger hurried up to the door and rang the bell hard—several times. He was carrying a doctor's bag and I thought it was an emergency. So I opened the door at once and right away he sprayed something from a bottle into my face.

That's all I remember. How did you happen to come down here?"

Captain Dana explained, then asked for a description of the caller. "I didn't get a good look at him," the doorman replied, "but he was about medium height and had a muscular build."

"That sounds like the man who snatched Aunt Harriet's purse," said Jean. "Did he have a beard?"

"No," the doorman replied.

"I'll bet he was wearing a false beard this afternoon," Jean thought.

"The fellow's clever," remarked Louise, "and very determined. I wonder if he'll try again."

"Not tonight, I'm sure," said Uncle Ned.

The doorman insisted he was all right and would guard the apartment until the relief man came on duty.

The Danas went upstairs and the girls told their aunt and cousin what had happened. Uncle Ned, meanwhile, reported the incident to the police. Then he turned to Cousin Cynthia.

"Now, my dear," he said, "I'll feel better after I go tomorrow if all of you move to a hotel."

Cousin Cynthia objected at once. "Harriet will be gone, too, and if the girls and I take special care until the lock is changed, I'm sure the intruder can't harm us again."

Aunt Harriet spoke up. "I can't understand what the man is after. Cynthia, do you have anything in this apartment really valuable?"

Mrs. Carson shook her head. "Nothing that should cause the man to be so violent. He must have some other motive. Could it have something to do with the Mr. Denver you girls have been trying to find?"

The sisters looked puzzled. "I don't see how it could," said Louise. "So far as we know, Denver isn't aware we suspect him."

The group finally went back to bed but were up early the next morning to have Sunday breakfast and go to church together. Uncle Ned was sailing at noon and Aunt Harriet was flying to Oak Falls directly after lunch. Both were full of warnings to their nieces.

After the three had said good-by to Miss Dana at the airport, Cousin Cynthia announced that she would take the girls to Greenwich Village to meet the Wax Queen.

"At last!" Louise teased. "I was beginning to think we were never going there."

Mrs. Carson laughed. "Have we had time?" she countered.

Jean spoke up. "On the way, I hope you'll tell us all about her and the mystery."

"No need," Cousin Cynthia said, smiling. "You'll see for yourself now."

A taxi took them to a narrow street, lined with old-fashioned shops and houses. At one store, which had no name on it, Mrs. Carson told the driver to stop. She paid him and the three crossed the narrow sidewalk to the shop. Cousin Cynthia pushed a button and a bell rang inside.

"The place is always locked," she explained to the girls.

The door was opened by a wizened old man wearing black Oriental-type trousers and jacket. He was very stooped and had thinning white hair which reached almost to his shoulders.

"Hello, Osmo," Mrs. Carson said cheerfully. "These are my cousins, Louise and Jean Dana."

The elderly man smiled as he led the visitors into the dimly lighted shop. "I am very glad to meet you," he said in a low tone. Then, closing the door softly, he pointed toward a curtained doorway at the rear. "Sh!" Osmo whispered. "She's in a trance now. We cannot disturb her."

Jean and Louise wondered if he meant the Wax Queen. They could hear a woman mumbling.

What a strange place this was—old-fashioned in every respect, except for a giant air-conditioning unit, which seemed incongruous in these surroundings. As Osmo withdrew to stand beside the curtained doorway, the girls gazed around the room. The two side walls were lined with wide shelves filled with busts and statues. These were beautifully modeled in tan, peach, and black, and the Danas presumed they were made of wax.

"I don't see Queen Victoria anywhere," said Jean.

"No, but look at that lovely one." Louise

pointed to the figure of a slender woman in Egyptian robes. It had been done in a soft olive shade. Curious about her identity, Louise and Jean tiptoed across the room and read the name carved into the wax.

"Queen Nefertiti!" Louise murmured. "Isn't she beautiful?"

The sisters went back to their cousin. "Who made these statues and are they for sale?" Jean asked in a low tone.

Mrs. Carson nodded toward the rear room. "The woman in there makes and sells them."

"You mean she's a sculptress?" Louise queried.

"Yes. She is the Wax Queen. I think she is probably the most famous wax artist in the world today. She is very modest and keeps to herself a good part of the time. She is unusual, but you will like her, I'm sure."

Louise asked how the woman happened to be called the Wax Queen. Mrs. Carson explained that the title had been given to her by a member of a royal family whose portrait she had fashioned in wax. "She never goes by her real name. In fact, I do not know what it is. She is always addressed as the Wax Queen."

The girls' interest in the woman was mounting. How soon would she see them? Finally the mumbling in the next room ceased. Osmo said he would find out if she would permit her visitors to

"Sh!" Osmo whispered. "She's in a trance."

come in. He disappeared behind the curtain while the others waited eagerly.

A few minutes later he reappeared. "The Wax Queen will see you now," he said with a low bow.

He held the curtain aside and the three callers walked in. The throne was empty and the woman was standing with her back to them, removing her crown. As she placed it on a table, Osmo made the introductions.

"How do you do, Mrs. Carson?" said the Queen. "I'm glad to see you again, and pleased that you have brought your cousins. It is a pleasure to meet you young ladies."

The Dana girls were speechless. The Wax Queen was the woman who had tried to stop Mr. Denver at the Penfield Carnival!

CHAPTER VI

The ESP Message

"Oh!" the Wax Queen said, her face flushing in embarrassment. "You stare at me as if I were not of this earth. I assure you I am just a mortal—even though I do have ESP."

"ESP?" said Louise. "You mean extrasensory perception?"

The woman nodded. "Yes. Often I know what other people are thinking—that's mental telepathy, of course—and sometimes I have precognition, the ability to see the future."

"Can you do these things any time you want to?" Louise asked.

"No, but it is easier for me to receive knowledge if I go into deep concentration. I can't explain exactly what happens," she went on with a little frown, "but I will get a feeling that something is coming on me—a mental image or voices, even just an impression. For want of a better word, I call it a message."

"Has anyone ever explained how ESP works?" Jean asked.

The Queen smiled. "Not really. Some scientists are investigating the subject, though." Suddenly she said, "The psychic power I have must show in my face, for you looked amazed when you saw me."

Jean spoke up quickly. "We didn't mean to be rude. The reason we were staring is that we recognized you from the Penfield carnival. You tried to stop Mr. Denver from letting a girl draw the lucky number out of the barrel."

It was the Wax Queen's turn to stare. "Penfield, you say? I was never in Penfield in my life."

"But—" Jean began.

The Queen interrupted. "The woman you saw must have been my twin sister. We look very much alike."

As the sculptress paused and gazed into space, the girls thought of the note they had received. Jean was about to ask if the Queen's sister was Winifred Moffat, when the woman said, almost as if talking to herself, "So she is after him, too!"

The Danas and their cousin exchanged puzzled glances. Louise ventured to ask what the Wax Queen meant.

"The episode you saw in Penfield has a direct bearing on the mystery I would like you to solve."

The girls waited expectantly for her to go on. As she seemed about to speak again, Osmo appeared and said, "Dear Queen, I must go home soon. Do you wish me to show these young ladies the wax room before I leave?"

"Oh, yes." The Queen motioned to her guests. "Will you all go with Osmo, please? You may leave your coats in the closet here." She pointed to a heavy, old-fashioned door. "I feel another message coming to me which may help settle one of the problems. I must concentrate now."

After the visitors had hung up their coats, Osmo ushered them through the door at the rear into a good-sized, windowless room with a large skylight. Against the long rear wall was a stainless-steel counter with several big shiny containers at one end.

"Those are the melting pots," Osmo said. "There's an electrical heating unit in the counter under them." Then he nodded toward a corner. "Over there in the floor is the warm wax pit where we keep large quantities of liquid wax. Be careful!" he cautioned quickly as the girls followed him. "The floor is slippery."

Layers of spilled and hardened wax had made the rough concrete floor treacherous. Jean peered into one of the open pots. "Umm—smells nice."

"Beeswax—the finest there is," said Osmo. He pointed to wall shelves stacked with blocks of white wax. "It comes like that. I melt the wax and let it stand until the consistency is just right for the Queen to handle."

"How smooth and white it is!" said Louise.

"Not in the hive," Osmo declared. "There it's brown. But before the wax is sold, it is bleached in the sun and rain until it's milk white. Of course there are all kinds of waxes and many uses for them." He pointed to Jean's purse. "You polish that with a wax, I'll bet."

Mrs. Carson glanced at a basket on the counter. It was filled with wax heads and hands.

Osmo flicked them with his finger. "Discards, all to be melted down."

"They look so real," Louise observed with a shiver. "How does she achieve such lifelike skin tones?"

"A-ah." Osmo smiled wisely. "Only the Queen knows that. Waxworking is an old art and the mixtures of waxes and pigments have always been a secret. In Italy they were handed down from father to son."

He next pointed to a row of bottles on a shelf above the counter. "There are the colors she uses for painting the faces and clothes." He picked up one. "Gold dust," he whispered. "Sometimes she sprinkles it in the wax to make it shimmer."

Suddenly the old man's eyes gleamed. "Would you like to see Ugly Emma?" He whisked open a drawer and lifted out the wax head of a girl with a blurred-looking face and real hair covering only one side of her head.

"Each hair is inserted separately with a hot needle," Osmo explained. "But this poor girl was left in the sun and she melted. That's why she hasn't been finished." He patted the head affectionately and put it away.

"What about wax dolls?" Jean asked. "Our grandmother had one."

"Oh, yes," Osmo said. "The Italian ones were especially beautiful! But many a little girl cried over a melted face. Unfortunately, the dolls couldn't be played with in summer. Instead, they were well wrapped, put in airtight boxes, and stored in a cool place.

"Now look here!" Osmo darted across the floor to a panel of photographs on the wall near the wax pit. As the girls and their cousin hurried after him, Jean slipped. With a cry she skidded toward the well of liquid wax.

Louise seized her sister's arm, but too late! Jean fell, pulling Louise with her.

Mrs. Carson screamed as the two landed at the edge of the pit. Jean's arms flew out and her hands and purse splashed into the deep well of warm liquid.

For a moment both girls and their cousin were breathless with shock. Then Mrs. Carson started toward them.

"Stay there!" Louise warned as she and Jean sat

up. "The floor slants a little here and it's slick as ice!"

Carefully they stood up and walked gingerly to their cousin who held out her hands to them.

"Thank you, Louise," Jean said with a shaky laugh. "You saved me from a wax bath!"

Osmo had not moved. "That would have been too bad," he said with a chuckle. The visitors wondered at the man's odd sense of humor.

Chuckling again, he pointed to her dripping purse, rapidly turning white as the wax cooled. "You won't have to put any more on that!"

Jean grimaced. "No. I'll be peeling it off." As the wax grew firmer, Jean removed it from her hands and bag.

Meanwhile, Osmo led them to the panel of photographs he had started to show them before. "These are wax funeral effigies," he announced cheerfully. "When a Roman nobleman died, a wax figure of him was carried in his funeral procession. The custom lasted many centuries. See!" He pointed to several full-length figures in costume. "Queen Elizabeth I, Queen Anne, Lord Nelson. All these figures are in Westminster Abbey!"

"They look so natural," Jean remarked.

Osmo opened his eyes wide. "Oh, it is amazing what can be done with wax." He pointed to two doors at the left end of the room. "One of those rooms," he said, "is where the Queen makes her lifelike statues—in secret! Usually she keeps both doors locked and rarely lets anyone into her studio."

"Why does she work in seclusion?" Jean asked.

Osmo hunched his stooped shoulders. "I think it is because her ESP tells her what to do."

Louise smiled. "Judging from the statues we saw outside, she must get very good advice."

The girls became serious again, wondering if there were some other reason why the Wax Queen locked Osmo out of her studio? Didn't she trust him?

"What's behind the other door?" asked Jean.

Osmo explained that old and valuable wax pieces were kept in the room. Rarely did the sculptress show them.

"Is Queen Victoria in there?" Jean asked.

"Yes," Osmo answered. A frightened look crept over his face. "One morning I opened the front door and there she sat big as life on a shelf! Nobody knows how she got here or why."

His lips shut tight as he turned abruptly and led them back into the anteroom.

The Wax Queen sat on a couch. She looked extremely worried. "I received the message. It was an answer to how Queen Victoria got here. She was stolen!"

"Stolen!" Mrs. Carson exclaimed. "By whom? And from whom?"

The sculptress said that unfortunately the message had not provided any names. "What I am particularly worried about," she said, "is that I am harboring stolen goods."

"Shouldn't you call the police?" Cousin Cynthia asked quickly.

"Not yet," the Queen replied. "Under the circumstances, I think I had better call my lawyer for advice." Suddenly the sculptress spoke with spirit. "I don't want my name brought before the public in this connection. It could ruin my business!"

"I'm dreadfully sorry," said Mrs. Carson. "I know how upsetting it must be. The girls and I will leave now and come back tomorrow."

There was a long pause, then the Wax Queen looked up at her visitors. "No, I do not want you to go yet. For a moment I lost my head, but I'm all right now. I must show you Queen Victoria."

The sculptress arose and led the way to her private display room. She unlocked the door, stepped inside, and turned on an elegant old-fashioned ceiling lamp. The visitors hardly noticed the shelves of fine statues in white, amber, and black. The girls stood in the doorway, amazed at what they saw.

In the center of the room on a pedestal stood the bust of Queen Victoria. The wax figure was exquisite in texture and so finely delineated that the monarch looked as if she were about to speak.

There was the hint of a smile on the stately face, and the hair was combed gracefully around her temples. She wore a crown studded with jewels of various colors, which glittered and sparkled in the strong beam of light overhead.

"It's gorgeous!" Jean cried out, and Louise added, "It's the most beautiful statue I've ever seen."

"And the most finely molded *I* have ever seen," the Wax Queen told them. "I believe this bust is almost priceless. But why—oh why—did the thief leave it here?"

"That may be a very difficult mystery to solve," Louise remarked. "Is it what you wanted us to work on?"

The woman's eyes grew sad. "I have two mysteries for you. This is one of them."

Jean had walked forward to examine the Latin inscription etched into the base of the statue. " '*Imperii Nostra Regina*,' " she read. "That means '*Our Queen of the Empire*.' "

"I hope she was a happier queen than I am," said the sculptress. "I am in deep trouble. You girls must try to help me!"

As the sculptress spoke, she seemed to become very tired and grew pale. Suddenly she put one hand to her head and began to sway. Fearful that she was about to faint, Louise and Jean assisted her to the couch in the anteroom. After a few minutes, the sculptress' color returned and she smiled.

"I am all right now." The callers were relieved and said they must go.

This time the Wax Queen made no objection. "I will look forward to seeing you tomorrow when I will tell you about the other mystery."

Mrs. Carson and the girls got their coats and took a taxi back to the apartment house, where they found the bookcase still in place.

Cousin Cynthia looked at her watch. "It's just about time for the news," she said. "Louise, will you turn on the TV?"

She and the girls sat down to listen to the newscast. Suddenly they all leaned forward, startled by what the announcer was saying:

"The police have just revealed that a valuable wax bust of Queen Victoria has been stolen from the private collection of Mr. and Mrs. Philip Anderson."

Louise and Jean were thunderstruck. The Queen's ESP message had been correct! Then a second thought came to Louise.

Seeing the troubled expression on her sister's face, Jean asked what was the matter.

"You realize," said Louise, "that what she told us about having ESP might be a hoax. The Queen herself could be the thief!"

CHAPTER VII

A Sealed Secret

JEAN nodded thoughtfully. "I see what you mean, Louise."

"Well, I don't!" Cousin Cynthia leaned forward in her easy chair. "If the Wax Queen had stolen the bust, why should she call attention to the fact by pretending to get ESP information about it? Why should she tell me it was in her shop, or ask you girls to find out how it got there?"

"Because the bust is made of wax, it is probable that sooner or later the police will question her about the theft," Louise replied. "Then she will use us to establish her innocence."

"Of course!" Jean agreed. "We were there when she got the ESP message and we can vouch that she engaged us to find out how the bust got into her shop."

"But then why steal the statue at all?"

Mrs. Carson asked. "When the police see it, they'll return the statue to the owner."

Jean sighed. "It's a puzzle. Maybe the Queen only wanted to keep it a little while—perhaps to copy it."

Louise asked her cousin how she had become acquainted with the sculptress.

"I heard about her beautiful work and went there to buy a statue as a gift. The Wax Queen and I got to talking and I happened to mention that you girls like to solve mysteries. She said, 'Maybe your cousins would like to solve a couple for me.'"

"I rather liked her," Jean remarked. "It's hard to believe she's guilty."

Louise agreed. "But we must examine all the possibilities, even if they are unpleasant."

"What about Osmo?" asked Jean. "He could be the thief and is trying to throw suspicion on the Queen, or he might be her accomplice."

"It's possible," Louise agreed.

Cousin Cynthia sighed and smiled. "Girls, I've had enough detective work for one day. Let's go out to the kitchen and whip up some supper."

After the three had eaten a delicious shrimp salad with hot rolls, Louise called Oak Falls to be sure Aunt Harriet had arrived home safely. Miss Dana answered the phone.

Her niece asked how the trip was, then reported what they had learned that afternoon.

Miss Dana laughed. "I can see you didn't waste any time. By the way, I noticed some posters advertising a carnival to be held here Tuesday. A beautiful sports car will be awarded to the holder of the lucky number. I thought Mr. Denver might possibly be in charge."

Louise requested her aunt to find out and to let the girls know. "If he is there, we'd like to be at that carnival and see what happens."

Miss Dana laughed. "And leave your New York mystery?"

"It doesn't take long to fly to Oak Falls," Louise replied. "From what the Wax Queen said, we know there is a connection between Denver and one of her mysteries."

Her aunt chuckled. "Do you think you will have all your puzzles solved by the end of your vacation?" she teased.

"Just try us!" Louise declared with a laugh.

She reported the conversation to her sister and cousin. "Make whatever plans you wish, but count me out tomorrow morning," Cousin Cynthia told the girls. "I want to be here when the locksmith comes."

The following morning Louise and Jean took a taxi to the Wax Queen's shop. Osmo opened the door, but this time he did not have a welcoming smile.

"Good morning, young ladies," he said, leading

them inside. "I am glad you have come. Perhaps you can help us. Something dreadful has happened."

"To the Wax Queen?" Louise asked quickly.

"No, thank goodness, but to Queen Victoria. She was stolen last night!"

The girls exchanged glances. Was Louise's theory true? Could this be the next step in a hoax?

Osmo explained that the sculptress had not left her studio until after ten o'clock. "Then she locked the door and went upstairs to her apartment. You know she lives above the shop," he added.

The elderly man said that the shop door had not been forced and there were no windows, so he did not see how anyone could have entered.

"What about the back door?" Jean asked.

"There is none," he replied. "There used to be one in the wax room, but the Queen had it sealed off with a new back wall when she installed the counter. She put in small ventilators instead."

"Perhaps someone used a skeleton key to get in," Louise suggested.

"Possibly," Osmo replied, "but the door to the shop has a kind of lock that a skeleton key is not supposed to open."

"Who are the people who do have keys to the shop?" Louise asked.

Osmo said no one did except the Queen and himself. "She once told me she had another one hidden in her apartment, but she didn't say where." Seeing how distraught the elderly man was, Louise and Jean found it hard to believe that he was guilty of any wrongdoing. They did not feel so confident about the Wax Queen. She could well have a confederate who had entered the shop and taken the bust. Or she might have removed it herself.

The girls thought of another possibility. The woman could be innocent, and the same person who had stolen the bust from the Anderson collection might have taken it from the shop.

Neither girl made any comment to Osmo, except to express their sympathy that he and the sculptress were having all this trouble.

"Where's the Wax Queen now?" Louise asked.

Osmo said that she was working in her studio. He smiled faintly. "Whenever the Queen has a problem and the answer does not come immediately by ESP, she goes to her studio and starts sculpting like mad. That seems to relieve her mind."

Jean spoke up. "I suppose we couldn't go in to watch her?"

Osmo replied, "She said to make an exception for you, so you may. But don't disturb her."

The girls put their coats in the closet. Then they tiptoed across the wax room, careful not to skid. Through the open door of the Queen's studio, they saw the sculptress sitting on a high stool, her back to them. Before her on a square pedestal was a partly finished bust. The room was lit by a small skylight and even in the clear light of day the flesh-colored wax looked almost real. The Wax Queen was so intent on her work that she did not seem to be aware of the girls' presence.

The Danas were amazed at the artist's dexterity. Apparently she had to work fast before the wax hardened. As she leaned back to examine the bust, Jean and Louise got a good view of the head.

Surprised, Jean forgot that she was to remain quiet. In a loud whisper, she said, "Why, Louise, that's a statue of you!"

At this, the sculptress turned around, startled. "Oh!" she said. The girls at once looked a little sheepish, but the Queen smiled at them.

"I knew all the time you were here," she said. "I could feel your presence. But you did surprise me when you spoke."

The visitors gazed at the wax figure on the pedestal. "It's marvelous!" Louise said. "But how in the world did you make it without a model?"

The Wax Queen laughed. "Oh, that's easy," she said. "I have a photographic memory and whenever I look at people I study their features in great detail. Later I can shut my eyes and see exactly what I need to know."

"Did you do it all this morning?" Jean asked.

"Oh no," the sculptress replied. "This is not the

first bust of Louise I have made. There were two others." She chuckled. "They were no good, so I had Osmo melt them down."

Suddenly the Queen said, "Has Osmo told you about Queen Victoria disappearing?"

"Yes," said Louise. "Have you notified the police?"

"No!" the woman exclaimed quickly. "I cannot do that!"

"But why not?" Jean asked.

"I haven't called my lawyer yet," said the Queen. "I must do that first."

Suddenly she stood up. "I forgot!" she exclaimed. "My ESP has brought me news about you."

The Danas sensed that she intended to say no more about the missing statue.

"Good or bad news?" Jean asked.

"Very good. While you are visiting your cousin, you are going to have a delightful surprise."

"What is it? the sisters asked excitedly.

The sculptress shook her head. "If I tell you, it won't be a surprise. Some other people are involved in it and they wouldn't like the surprise spoiled. What I have done is write this out on paper and put it into a sealed envelope. You are to give it to Mrs. Carson."

No amount of coaxing could get the secret out of the Wax Queen. She reached into a pocket of her smock, pulled out an envelope, and handed it to Louise. "Promise me you won't open it until I give you permission," she said, a twinkle in her eyes.

"I promise."

The sculptress continued to gaze at Louise. Then she stared at the wax head of the girl. Finally she said, "The ears are wrong. I must do them over. Will you please call Osmo and tell him to bring me a little hot wax."

At once Jean said, "Can't I do it?"

The woman hesitated. "All right, but watch out for Caesar—my cat. He doesn't like strangers."

Jean went into the big room and walked over to one of the vats in which there was flesh-colored liquid wax. Sitting on a shelf above the counter was a large black cat. With unblinking yellow eyes and tail twitching, he watched Jean fill a long-handled dipper. Then, when she started for the studio, he gave a loud hiss and leaped across her path. With a gasp Jean stopped short and skidded.

The dipper tilted and hot wax splashed onto her leg. Jean cried out in pain!

CHAPTER VIII

The Problem Brother

HEARING Jean's cry of pain, Louise and the Wax Queen rushed to her side.

"Oh dear!" the sculptress exclaimed. "You're burned! I'm so sorry! I will get something for you right away!"

She dashed across the big room and picked up a can of powder from a shelf. In the meantime, Louise had helped Jean remove her stocking, which was full of holes and had wax clinging to it.

The sculptress returned with the powder and sprinkled it generously over Jean's leg. "That will soothe the burn and keep you from getting an infection. Osmo and I often get little burns while working and we have found this very effective." After a pause, she said, "However, if you think you should go to a doctor, I will be glad to pay for it."

"That won't be necessary," Jean replied. "It feels better." She asked the Queen please to go on with her work. Louise then refilled the dipper with hot wax and took it into the studio, where she set it down beside the statue of herself.

The sculptress seated herself again on the high stool and gently poured some of the liquid wax over the area of the ears. In a short time it congealed. Then, deftly, with her fingers and tools, she shaped two ears that were a perfect copy of Louise's own.

The Queen got up and walked off a little distance to survey her handiwork. In a moment she smiled. "Now I am satisfied. It is such a joy to be able to turn out a real likeness."

"It must be," said Louise. "I don't see how you do it." She gave a little chuckle. "You know, it almost scares me looking at that. It's like meeting yourself face to face!"

The sculptress, in a particularly happy mood, became quite talkative. She told the girls about various men and women in public life whose likenesses she had fashioned in wax. Louise and Jean wondered when she was going to get to the subject of the mystery.

Finally Jean could wait no longer. She asked abruptly, "Queen, is your real name Moffat?"

The sculptress gave a start. She looked at Jean piercingly and did not answer at once. But finally she said, "Yes. My maiden name was Moffat—Wendy Moffat. My twin sister is Winnie—Winifred Moffat. She is the one you saw at Penfield. But how in the world did you know the name?"

Louise and Jean told her about the special-delivery letter they had received at school and the instructions in it.

"I see," the sculptress said, gazing at the floor and blinking as if lost in thought. Then she looked up. "Strange, isn't it? Unknown to each other, I and my sister have both asked you for help. Well," she went on, "I will tell you the story.

"Mr. Denver is our brother—that's an assumed name, of course. Quite by accident Winnie found out he was using that name. Fred was always jealous of us girls, feeling that our parents favored us over him. This wasn't true, of course. He was very headstrong, and he disliked me because often I could read his mind. I'd tell him that what he was planning to do would get him into trouble.

"Finally Fred ran **away** from home. I didn't see him for years—in fact, not until after my husband's death. Bill had no use for Fred. Since my husband's death, though, Fred has come here several times, threatening me."

Louise spoke up. "Threatening you? Why?"

A look of sadness came into the Wax Queen's eyes. "Fred keeps insisting that I sell him my business and all the wax figures. He wants to pay me only a very small sum, but as you can see, these figures are worth a great deal."

"Does he still come?"

The sculptress said that he had not been there in the past few weeks. "I decided to keep the door locked and Osmo was instructed not to let Fred come in."

Jean asked, "And yet you want to find your brother?"

The Queen nodded. "I can never tell when he will turn up again. It's very uncomfortable living with this shadow over me. At times it interferes with my work. Besides, Fred owes my sister Winnie a large sum of money and he should be made to pay it. She and I have a lawyer who has been trying to locate him, but without success. I thought an attorney might be able to scare Fred into leaving me alone." The sculptress smiled. "I haven't told the lawyer I was going to ask two schoolgirls to locate my brother."

"I hope we can solve this mystery for you," said Louise. "As a matter of fact, we do have a possible lead."

"You have?" the Queen asked hopefully.

Louise said that it was a slim chance. She explained about their aunt having told them there was to be a carnival in Oak Falls and that it was likely her brother would be in charge of awarding the car to a lucky winner.

"Oh, this is marvelous information," the Queen said excitedly. "I must tell Osmo about it at once." She rushed out.

Louise and Jean were interested to see that the woman confided in Osmo. "She must trust him," Jean said. "What do you think of the two of them now?"

"I think the Queen is sincere about wanting to find her brother, but as for the stolen bust—I still don't know."

"Shall we tell her our suspicion about Denver?" Jean asked.

"Wait," said her sister, "until we are sure we're right."

While waiting for the sculptress, they walked around the bust of Louise admiring it more each time they noticed another detail.

"I can understand now," said Jean, "how Wendy Moffat got the name of the Wax Queen."

As she spoke, the doorbell rang. Moments later a cry came from the shop. The girls rushed out to the front room. There stood a burly man with whiskers. His coat collar was turned up and a felt hat was pulled low over his face. He was twisting the Wax Queen's wrist. As she moaned in pain, Osmo darted from a corner with a large statue in his hand.

"Stop that!" he cried, and with full force brought the heavy piece down onto the man's wrist. With a yelp of pain, the intruder let go. At that instant he saw the girls rushing toward him and dashed out the door.

Louise and Jean ran into the street and looked up and down. He was gone! But a car sped away from the curb a few doors down and they surmised he was in it.

"That was the man who snatched Aunt Harriet's purse!" exclaimed Jean. "I recognized him even with his face partly hidden."

"So did I," said Louise. "I wonder who he is."

"Maybe the Queen knows," Jean replied.

They asked her, but she declared she had never seen him before.

"What did he want and why did he grab your wrist?" Louise asked.

The sculptress was shivering. "He mumbled something. It sounded like 'You've got to sell this shop to your brother or you'll be sorry.' Then he grabbed me."

"He must be in your brother's employ," Jean said.

"I agree," replied the Queen. Sadly she added, "I owe much to Osmo, my faithful friend." She extended her hand to the elderly man and he patted it. The Danas felt certain that the assistant was not involved in the double theft of the bust. Obviously he was loyal and would do nothing to hurt the woman or cast suspicion on her. They wished they could feel as certain of the Queen's honesty.

"Girls," said the sculptress, "I am tired now. Come back tomorrow and—"

Louise and Jean waited for her to finish the sentence, but suddenly she became starey-eyed and was completely lost in thought. Gently they led her to the couch in the anteroom and then put on their coats. They intended to leave the Queen without trying to say good-by, but as they started through the curtain, she called, "Wait!" They stopped abruptly.

"I have just had a message," she said. "It was vague, but it means harm is coming to you girls. I will concentrate on warding it off."

"Can you actually keep this harm from happening?" Jean asked, amazed.

"I don't know," the Queen replied humbly. "I can only try. My thoughts will be with you, but you must be very careful. You are in great danger!"

CHAPTER IX

A Near Crash

WHEN the girls left the shop, Jean asked worriedly, "Do you think we are in danger? Or is the Wax Queen fooling us?"

"I wish we knew," said Louise. "I can't figure her out. Sometimes she seems lovely, then at others she is just plain queer. I'm sure there is something in her mind she's not telling us, otherwise she would have got in touch with the police about Queen Victoria."

Jean agreed. "There's no way of knowing whether she really gets those ESP messages, but I must admit I have butterflies in my stomach." Then she added with a wry smile, "Being warned of danger kind of shakes one up."

Louise laughed. "I know. And I don't think we can put much faith in the Wax Queen being able to ward off the trouble for us."

"The whole thing gives me the shivers," said Jean.

The two girls kept alert as they strolled along the narrow Greenwich Village streets. They decided to take a bus back to their cousin's apartment.

"Let's not tell her about the Wax Queen's warning," Louise suggested.

Jean nodded. "After all, it may be a fraud."

When the girls arrived they found a brand-new lock on the apartment door.

Cousin Cynthia let them in and gave them keys for it. Then Louise handed her the sealed envelope from the Wax Queen and explained what it was.

Mrs. Carson raised her eyebrows. "I can hardly wait to find out what's in it! By the way," she added, "I was just looking in the newspaper to see if there was any word about the Queen Victoria bust."

"Is there?" Louise asked.

"Just that it was stolen over a week ago, but the owners withheld the news, preferring to make a private investigation."

Louise sat down, looking very serious. "You both know we're in a spot, don't you?"

Jean nodded. "We ought to tell the police what we know, but it will put the Queen in a bad light if we do. She should inform them herself."

The girls told their cousin of the new developments.

Mrs. Carson frowned. "It almost looks as if the woman is guilty."

"But we must give her the benefit of the doubt," said Louise. Then she brightened. "When the Queen talks to her lawyer, I think he will advise going to the police. If he doesn't, and she still refuses, we'll have to do it ourselves."

"Let's call the Queen and urge her to contact the lawyer at once," said Jean. But they could not find her in the telephone book under the names Moffat or Wax Queen, nor was she listed in the classified directory under the commercial "wax" headings.

"She's probably listed under her married name and we don't know what that is!" Louise pointed out. She turned to Jean. "You and I are slipping!"

"We sure are!" her sister said.

Cousin Cynthia laughed. "Agreed," she said. "You've both become entirely too serious. I have a nice surprise for you. For a change you are going to have some fun and forget these mysteries."

"What's going on?" Jean asked.

"Sailboat races!" said Mrs. Carson. "On Long Island Sound this afternoon there are to be special races. I have a friend who owns a yacht. Right now it is moored out on the Hudson River. He has invited us to come aboard and go with him."

"Marvelous!" Jean exclaimed excitedly.

Cousin Cynthia went on, "He has a speedboat which will take us out to the yacht."

The thought of the races thrilled the girls. They quickly changed into slacks, shirts, and windbreakers. In the meantime, Mrs. Carson brought out tasty sandwiches she had made earlier and the three sat down to a quick lunch. As they ate, they talked over details of the coming trip.

Suddenly Louise said, "Sh-h!" They listened and heard a board creak outside the kitchen door. Louise tiptoed over, quietly turned the lock, and flung it open. A tall, lanky man was leaning against the jamb, eavesdropping! With a gasp he took to his heels and ran down the stairway. Louise dashed after him while Jean rang for the elevator to try to reach the first floor before they did. No use! By the time the girls met in the lobby, the man had left the building.

"Nobody went out but the messenger," the doorman told them. "He had a telegram for the Smiths."

A call to the Smiths on the house phone confirmed the Danas' suspicion. No telegram had been delivered.

Louise told the doorman what had happened.

"But what could I do?" the man protested. "He showed me the telegram and I was busy on the phone so I let him go up!"

The girls hurried back to the apartment.

Mrs. Carson was upset. "I don't like this. If that man was really eavesdropping, he knows our plans." Then she tried to shake off her mood.

"But we'll just have to keep alert. No use fussing. It will spoil our whole afternoon. Let's leave."

As the Danas and their cousin went out to the street, two taxis came along. They hailed the first one and got in. A man wearing dark glasses was standing at the curb. He took the second one. As they drove toward the river, Louise said, "I believe that taxi is following us."

Their driver, a cheerful round-faced young man, commented, "Oh, don't be worried, ladies."

Louise smiled, and thought perhaps this was good advice. But when they reached the pier where the speedboat was moored, the man in the taxi behind them got out, too, and she was not so sure their driver was right. The stranger was a clean-shaven, muscular man of medium height. He did not speak, but stood to one side and the Danas sensed he was watching them from behind the dark glasses.

The yacht owner, a distinguished-looking, white-haired man, greeted Mrs. Carson and she presented him to the girls. "I am so glad you could come," Mr. Hooper said. After a few minutes' conversation, he helped them into the boat. As Mr. Hooper revved the motor, the girls noticed that the man with the sunglasses had disappeared.

The speedboat shot away from the dock and headed straight for the yacht in the middle of the river. "We're happy to come along," said Louise to their host. "Your yacht is beautiful!"

"Mrs. Hooper and I enjoy it. We take long cruises in it."

The words were hardly out of his mouth when another speedboat crossed directly in front of him.

"You crazy pilot!" Mr. Hooper shouted.

He swung the wheel of his own craft hard to the left, trying to avoid a collision. The turn was so abrupt and unexpected that both Louise and Jean lost their balance and tumbled overboard!

Icy water engulfed the girls. Gasping, they bobbed to the surface and were hauled aboard.

Mr. Hooper had stopped the speedboat and apologized to the shivering girls. They assured him the accident was not his fault.

"We might have had a crash," Mrs. Carson said nervously. She had been thrown to the deck, but fortunately had only a couple of bruises from her fall.

"I'll get you to the yacht right away and Mrs. Hooper will find you some dry clothes," their host said.

His wife, a quiet, gracious person, immediately took the girls below and supplied them with temporary outfits. While the sisters were changing, Louise remarked, "Well, I guess the Wax Queen was right that something was going to happen to us."

"Yes," said Jean "and who knows—maybe her thoughts for our safety kept the accident from being worse."

"I feel sure," said Louise, "that the near collision was deliberate. I'll bet the man who followed us in the taxi was at the wheel of the other speedboat."

Jean agreed. "He might have been the purse snatcher minus his whiskers—the man who threatened the Queen this morning. He was about the same age and build."

"Too bad none of us caught the name or the registration number of his boat."

When the girls appeared on deck again, their cousin said, "Let's put the accident and mysteries out of our minds for the time being."

"Good idea!" said Mr. Hooper. "We just want you to enjoy this trip!"

Louise and Jean smiled and promised to forget their detective work.

Mr. Hooper then sent the speedboat back to shore by one of the crew and the yacht sailed down the Hudson.

Each time they saw the New York skyline, the Danas were more amazed at its growth. "Tall glass buildings are popping up all over," Jean commented.

"I'm fascinated by your yacht, Mr. Hooper," said Louise. "It goes much faster than my uncle's ocean liner!"

Mr. Hooper laughed. "My craft makes good time," he said and added, "We have a lovely day for our trip."

Louise and Jean tumbled overboard

The sun was bright and a fresh breeze ruffled the girls' hair. It seemed that in no time they were at Long Island Sound watching the races.

"How beautiful it is!" Louise exclaimed. "All those bright-colored sails against the blue water!"

"And just see how the boats whiz around the buoys!" put in Jean. "There are so many different classes!"

People watching from anchored boats applauded the winners enthusiastically.

When the races were over, the Hooper yacht returned to the Hudson River. After thanking their host and hostess, Mrs. Carson and the girls went back to shore in the speedboat, then took a taxi. During the ride Louise and Jean talked about the races. Presently they noticed that their cousin had not said a word. She was looking straight ahead, lost in thought.

When they reached the apartment she still had not spoken and finally Louise asked her if she was feeling all right.

"Yes," she said, "but I am frightened. I have been mulling over an idea ever since our near crash. My dears, I don't want to seem inhospitable, but there is too much chance of something happening to you in New York. I believe you'd better go home and come to visit me another time."

The girls were stunned. Leave New York before the mysteries were solved?

CHAPTER X

A Tricky Intrusion

ALTHOUGH Louise and Jean were amazed and disappointed by Mrs. Carson's suggestion that they go home, the girls were too polite to argue the matter with her. But they could not disguise their glumness.

Cousin Cynthia regarded them thoughtfully. Suddenly she smiled. "Does solving these mysteries really mean so much to you that you're willing to take a chance on staying in New York?"

"Yes," the girls answered simultaneously.

"Well, then, I guess I'll have to change my mind," their cousin said. "But I'm going to keep right on worrying about you. As often as I can do it, I'll stay with you."

At that moment the telephone rang. "Please answer it, Louise," said her cousin. "You're closest."

Louise picked up the receiver. "Hello."

There was a momentary pause before the caller answered. Then a woman said, "Who's this? One of the Dana girls?"

"This is Louise." She thought the voice was the Wax Queen's, but it was so strained that she could not be sure.

"I'm in dreadful trouble!" the woman exclaimed. "Please come down to my shop right away!"

"Who is this?" Louise asked.

"Don't you know me? I'm the Wax Queen, of course."

"I want to be sure," Louise said. "Give me some sign of your identity."

"Why—uh—what I want to talk to you about is Victoria. She's still missing."

Louise did not want to sound cool, if it really was the Wax Queen, but she thought that this might be a hoax to lead the Danas into a trap. "Tell me something else," she requested.

"Louise, what has happened?" the caller asked. "I'm the Wax Queen. Don't you remember I made a bust of you?"

"I guess that's enough proof," Louise replied. "We'll be right down."

"Oh, thank you," the Wax Queen said. "Get here as quickly as you can." Louise hung up and relayed the message to her sister and cousin.

In the excitement supper was forgotten. Mrs. Carson and the girls put on their coats, hurried downstairs, and hailed a taxi. When they reached the shop, it was dark.

"Oh, I hope nothing has happened to the Wax Queen!" Jean said fearfully.

She rang the bell. When no one answered, she rang a second time.

Mrs. Carson looked worried. "Maybe the Queen is lying in there—hurt." She began to pound on the door. There was no answer.

"Try the bell to the Queen's apartment," Louise suggested.

They stepped to the nearby door and both rang and knocked. Still no answer!

Jean said, "Let's call the police and—" She stopped short and pointed down the street. "There she is!"

"Sorry to keep you waiting," the sculptress said as she hurried up to them. "I have no phone, so I had to go outside to call you. Then I thought of a few errands I had to do." She tapped a large grocery bag she was carrying. "Let's go inside."

She unlocked the shop door, then flicked the wall switch. As they followed her, the sculptress suddenly gave a cry of dismay.

"What's the matter?" Jean asked.

With a trembling finger the Queen pointed to an empty section of a shelf. "Two pieces are missing!" she cried out. "Somebody has stolen them!"

"What was taken?" Louise asked. "Something

that could tie in with the Queen Victoria theft?"

"Two busts are gone—one of Napoleon Bonaparte and the other of Marie Antoinette."

"All three of the missing statues are of famous people," Louise reminded the sculptress. "Maybe the thief intends to sell them to a wax museum."

"Very likely," the Queen conceded. "But there are hundreds of museums all over the world. I doubt if the person would be foolish enough to dispose of them in this country."

"Nevertheless," Jean said, "the places can be checked, even if it takes a long time."

Mrs. Carson spoke up. "The first thing to do is to have the locks on your outside doors changed."

"I suppose so," the Queen said. "There's a locksmith down the street who stays open late. Would you girls run down and see if he could take care of it right away?"

The locksmith worked quickly, but by the time the job was done, the Danas and their cousin were starved. Mrs. Carson suggested that the Queen join them at a nearby Chinese restaurant. "We can talk over your trouble while we eat."

The Queen agreed. "First I must take the groceries up to the apartment."

"I'll do it," Louise offered. "Then we can stop by the police station and notify them of the thefts."

A frightened expression spread over the woman's face. "I can't do that."

"But you must!" Jean burst out. "Surely you want to recover the pieces. Besides, you can't keep quiet about Queen Victoria any longer!"

"If you don't tell," Louise said gently, "we will have to."

When she heard this, the Queen seemed to lose all her strength. She dropped into a chair and covered her face with her hands. She began to sob.

"Please don't cry," Louise said, putting an arm around the woman's shoulder.

"I can't help it," the sculptress replied. "The police are the last people in the world I want to see."

"Please tell us why," Louise begged.

"Because—because," the Queen answered, "I'm likely to be arrested any minute!"

Her listeners were shocked. The sculptress took her hands from her tear-stained face and added, "Someone has accused me of stealing the Victoria bust."

"Who?" Mrs. Carson asked.

"I don't know. Late this afternoon I received an anonymous letter. All it said was that the writer was tipping off the police I was the thief."

The Queen opened her handbag and brought out a typewritten note, which she gave them to read.

"I'm innocent," the woman went on, "but who will believe me? Only the recovery of the statue will exonerate me now. That is why I called you down here to help. I would do anything to get that statue back!"

Suddenly Louise's eyes flashed. "Of course you would!" she exclaimed. "And that tells us who stole the bust and why!"

The Queen and Cousin Cynthia were thunderstruck. But Jean was grinning. "See if I'm with you, Sis." She turned to the sculptress. "The note's probably from your brother. He figures that when you're in trouble with the police, he will offer to produce the statue, providing you sell him your business at his price."

"Of course!" said Cousin Cynthia. "That must be it! Unless," she said to the Queen, "you have other enemies?"

The woman shook her head. "No. The girls are right, I think."

The Danas urged her to go to the police and tell them the whole story, but the trembling woman begged for a little more time to get up her courage.

Louise frowned. "You ought to go to them before they come for you," she said.

"Perhaps after supper," Cousin Cynthia said kindly. She insisted that the Queen wash her face, put some powder on her nose, and come along to the restaurant. After Mrs. Carson had gone upstairs with her, Louise said, "I feel sure the Queen is innocent."

"I agree," Jean replied. "But is it still possible

that she is a marvelous actress playing an elaborate cover-up game?"

"No," said Louise, "she wouldn't write a note accusing herself. That's going too far!"

A few minutes later the foursome walked the short distance to the Chinese restaurant. They had hardly given their order, when the restaurant owner hastened up to them with a narrow wooden box in his hand.

"You are the Wax Queen?" he asked the sculptress. When she nodded, he handed her the box. It was tied with string. "I was asked to give this to you." He hurried off.

Mystified, the sculptress started to open the string. Suddenly Louise grabbed her arm.

"Don't do that!" she exclaimed. "There may be something dangerous inside!"

CHAPTER XI

A Gift Trap

For a moment the Queen stared at the box in her hand. Then she quickly put it on the table before her.

"You really think it could be dangerous?" she asked the Danas.

"There's no telling what's inside," Louise replied.

"You don't even know who sent it to you," Mrs. Carson said, looking worried.

As the Queen was about to reply, she glanced up and her face turned ashen. Coming in the door of the restaurant was a policeman. He walked straight toward their table.

"This is it," said the Wax Queen, her voice trembling.

To the amazement of all four, the officer strode past and entered the kitchen. The Queen heaved a sigh of relief.

"I'll tell you what," Jean said impetuously.

"I'm going to have the policeman examine this package. Come on, Louise!" She picked up the narrow box and hurried toward the kitchen. Jean excused herself and followed.

On the other side of the swinging door, the girls were met by the clatter of pots and the high-pitched chatter of the chefs and waiters.

The policeman stood talking to the owner, a short, thin Chinese. The owner hastened over. "Please, young ladies, not in the kitchen!"

"We would like to talk to the officer," said Jean.

The policeman heard her and approached the girls. "What's the trouble, miss?"

"We're here with a friend," said Jean, "and this package was just delivered to her. But we don't know who sent it. She has enemies and we are afraid of what might be inside. Would you open it for us?"

The policeman gazed at Jean with a searching look. "Young lady," he said, "if this is some kind of joke—"

Jean assured him that if it were, the woman to whom the box had been delivered did not think so. "Please take it," she pleaded.

"All right. The police station is the place to take care of this. You girls will have to come along."

"But first," said Louise, turning to the pro-prietor, "tell us who gave you the package."

Eyeing the box uneasily, the Chinese replied that a bearded man had stepped in the front door of the restaurant and placed the box beside the cash register. "I was on duty there. The fellow pointed out your friend and asked me to give it to her. Said he was in a hurry and left. Do you think there's something dangerous in it?" he asked nervously.

"We'll check on that now," the policeman said. "Come along," he added to the girls. "We'll go out the back and down the alley."

Jean followed him, but Louise hurried into the dining room and explained to her cousin and the Wax Queen where they were going. Then she joined her sister and the officer as they emerged from the alley.

The three walked the short distance to the police station, where the officer took the box into a back room. Louise and Jean were told to wait on a bench near the sergeant's desk.

Ten minutes later the officer looked out and beckoned the girls. They followed him into an office where a broad-shouldered man with crew-cut gray hair sat behind a large desk.

The officer introduced him as Captain Brown. After identifying themselves, the Danas told where they were staying in New York. The captain had them repeat their story of the box and studied them intently as they spoke.

"Who advised your friend not to open it?" he asked.

"I did," Louise replied.

The captain nodded approval. "Good thinking," he said. "Now I'll show you something."

Before him on the desk was the wooden box. The string had been removed. Captain Brown slid back the lid and poked inside with a pencil. There was a loud *snap!* When he withdrew the pencil, they saw that its end had been neatly sliced off.

Louise and Jean stared, horrified.

"Simple mechanism," Captain Brown commented grimly, "but devilish. It could have cost your friend a finger."

"How awful!" Louise murmured. "She might never have been able to make another statue."

"Statue?" Captain Brown said quickly. "What's your friend's name?"

For a moment the Danas hesitated. Then, knowing that they must answer, Louise said, "She is the Wax Queen. Her name is Mrs. Campbell."

Captain Brown's eyes narrowed and he reached for a typewritten paper on his desk. "Someone slipped this under the street door about half an hour ago. It is an anonymous note accusing her of theft."

"Yes, we know about it," Jean said anxiously. "We're quite sure someone is playing a malicious trick on her."

Captain Brown stood up. "Nevertheless, we'll have to bring her in for questioning. Officer Hobart, go back to the restaurant and get her."

The policeman moved toward the door.

The Danas jumped up. "We'll go with you," Louise said quickly. "Perhaps if we're there, she won't be so frightened!"

Meanwhile, at the restaurant, the Wax Queen was despondent. She pushed away the dish of delicious moo-goo-gai-pan.

"I'm sorry," she said. "I just can't eat a bite."

"It will do you good," coaxed Mrs. Carson. "Look at those lovely little pieces of chicken in there."

The sculptress shook her head. "I wish the girls had not gone to the police. They will tell who I am and I will be arrested."

"But if you are innocent, you have nothing to worry about," Cousin Cynthia said soothingly. She lectured the woman earnestly on why she ought to tell the police her story. "Then you'll have peace of mind," she concluded.

"And I need that badly," the sculptress agreed. "Without it, my ESP works poorly. As it is now, my mind is so cluttered with worry that I can't concentrate."

"Then you must do what I say," Mrs. Carson said firmly. "I promise you, it will help you. Why are you so afraid?"

The Wax Queen sighed. "You don't know how

hard I have worked to build my business. To be suspected of a theft—what a black mark that would be on my name!"

Mrs. Carson took her hand. "But don't you see that it will be worse for you if you don't go to the police yourself. It is the *only* thing to do."

For a long moment the Wax Queen stared at her plate. Then she squared her shoulders. "Yes, I see you are right. I will do it." Suddenly she gave a deep sigh. "Oh, I feel so much better! It is such a relief to have my mind made up!"

The sculptress ate a little food, drank some tea, and was talking easily to her companion by the time the fortune cookies were served. Smiling, the women broke open the crisp cakes and took out the small printed fortunes.

"What does yours say?" Mrs. Carson asked cheerfully.

The Wax Queen did not reply. Cynthia Carson looked up to see the woman staring into space. The cookie lay in her limp hand.

"Oh dear!" said Mrs. Carson. "She's in what Osmo calls a trance."

She watched her companion closely as low murmurs and sighs came from the woman's lips. Finally the Queen's eyes widened, then a normal look returned to them. She smiled wanly. "I'm all right now."

"Did you receive a message?" Cousin Cynthia asked anxiously.

"Yes!" Two spots of color burned the Queen's cheeks. "I know who stole Victoria and the other busts from my shop. I saw an image of the thief!" The woman paused and Mrs. Carson waited eagerly for her to go on. "Refrigerator," said the Queen.

Mrs. Carson stared in amazement. Then she decided that the Wax Queen was feverish. "I'll get you a cool cloth for your face, dear," she said, and hurried to the rear of the restaurant where she had noticed a tray of napkins beside a water dispenser.

But the tray was not there now. Mrs. Carson told a waiter, who went to the kitchen and returned with a damp napkin neatly folded on a plate. Mrs. Carson thanked him as she took it and started back toward her table. She stopped short with a gasp.

The Wax Queen was gone!

CHAPTER XII

The Missing Key

MRS. CARSON looked quickly around the restaurant. The Wax Queen was not in sight.

"You look for friend?" asked a Chinese waiter. He pointed toward the front door. "She go out very fast. Something wrong?"

"I hope not," replied Cousin Cynthia. She quickly paid the check and hurried out to the street.

The sculptress was not in sight, but Louise and Jean were coming around the corner with a policeman.

"Oh, I'm so glad to see you!" exclaimed Mrs. Carson, running toward them. She reported what had happened. "Where do you think the Queen has gone?"

"She didn't give you any hint?" Louise asked.

"No. I told you—her final word was 'refrigerator.' "

"Maybe she's gone home to her refrigerator,"

Jean said, "although that doesn't seem to make much sense."

"We'll look there," Officer Hobart decided. "We have to start somewhere. My orders are to bring her in, and I intend to do it."

As they hastened toward the Wax Queen's shop, the girls told their cousin what they had learned in the kitchen and at the police station.

"Who do you think the bearded man is?" Mrs. Carson asked.

"I think he works for the Queen's brother," Louise replied. "Probably Denver figured that if the Queen were injured by the trap and unable to work, she would sell him the shop."

"What a terrible man!" Mrs. Carson said with a shiver.

As she spoke, they reached the Queen's shop and Officer Hobart rang the bell of her apartment. There was no answer. He rang again, then pounded hard.

In a moment they heard footsteps coming slowly down the stairs. The lock turned and the door opened. The Queen stood there, white-faced.

"Oh!" she gasped, upon seeing the policeman.

"Now, my dear," Mrs. Carson said firmly, "remember what you decided."

"You shouldn't have run away," Louise said kindly. "There's nothing to be afraid of."

"But I didn't mean to run away," the Queen said. "I had to come here immediately to check what I just learned through my ESP. I intended to rejoin you and go to the police."

For a moment the officer looked nonplused. Then he straightened his shoulders and said briskly, "You are Mrs. Wendal Moffat Campbell?"

"Yes," said the Queen.

"You will come with me, please."

"Oh, but first I must show you something upstairs. I think I can prove who stole the busts from my shop and how it was done. Please believe me," she added.

"All right," said the officer, "but make it quick."

She led them upstairs, took a key from her purse, and unlocked the door.

"I was just getting ready to go in," she explained, "when you rang downstairs."

She led the way into a tastefully decorated living room. It was softly lighted by two alabaster lamps which had been left burning at each end of a red-velvet sofa.

"Now, Mrs. Campbell," said Officer Hobart, "suppose you explain what this is all about."

The Queen invited them to sit down and started to tell the policeman of her ESP powers.

"I heard about that," he said briefly. "Why did you come here?"

"Because I must check in my refrigerator before I can be sure the ESP message was correct," she replied. "Follow me."

Puzzled, and somewhat amused, the others

trailed her to the kitchen. The Queen flung open the refrigerator door.

"The message was right!" she exclaimed. "The key is gone!"

"What key?" Mrs. Carson asked. "Your refrigerator has no key."

The Wax Queen chuckled. She put her finger on a small prong under a shelf.

"I hung a key to my shop on that hook. It was the old key before the locks were changed. You can see someone has taken it."

"And your ESP told you who it was?" Louise asked.

The sculptress said that while concentrating she had had a mental image of a tall, thin man taking the key from the refrigerator. "But his face was blurred," she added, "and he talked sort of garbled —as if his mouth were full of pebbles."

Jean spoke up. "But you know who he is?"

Mrs. Campbell smiled. "I think so. His strange way of speaking is a good clue."

She explained that shortly before Queen Victoria had appeared, a man with the same kind of speech defect had come to the apartment looking for work. "He had good references with him as a window washer, so I let him in. I must say he left the windowpanes shining."

Louise and Jean said they were skeptical of his references. "They could have been forged," Louise added.

Mrs. Campbell admitted this was probably true. "It's apparent now that he came to get the key. He must have had a long search."

Jean smiled ruefully. "Maybe not. He could have gone to your refrigerator for a bottle of soda and discovered the key."

The Danas thought he was probably another hireling of the Queen's brother. Louise asked the Queen, "Who else has been to your apartment in the past few weeks?"

"No one except my sister Winnie—and my brother Fred." As she said this, the Queen's eyes snapped. "At that time, he made his usual demand that I sell him the shop and everything in it at a ridiculous price. I told him to get out and stay out."

"Mrs. Campbell," Officer Hobart said firmly, "you'll have to tell all this to Captain Brown. Let's go now."

The sculptress appealed to the girls and their cousin to come with her.

"Of course," said Louise. "We have things to tell the captain too."

Half an hour later they were seated in his office and the Wax Queen had told her story. The Danas followed with an account of their adventures and what they had surmised about the case.

The captain looked grave. "Your brother is a dangerous man," he said to the Queen. "And you are foolish—you should have come to me as soon as the Victoria bust appeared in your shop."

"I know," the woman said humbly. "These girls have been urging me to tell you everything."

Captain Brown smiled as he regarded the Danas. "From what you've told me, I'd say you are certainly competent sleuths."

The two girls blushed and Cousin Cynthia spoke up promptly. "Indeed they are," she said proudly, and told him of some of the cases which the girls had solved.

The captain nodded, impressed. "What do you think of this one?" he asked the Danas.

Louise repeated their theory that Moffat, alias Denver, had staged the two thefts of Victoria to maneuver his sister into a bad position with the police. "Had it worked," said Louise, "he would have managed to return Victoria and thus exonerate his sister without implicating himself. But in return she would have had to give him her shop."

"And the other two busts?" the captain asked.

"Those he probably plans to sell to a museum," Louise replied.

Jean spoke up. "He has at least two accomplices: the burly bearded man and the tall one who posed as the window washer. The attacks on us mean that Denver knows we're after him."

"I agree," the captain said crisply. "On all counts!" He leaned forward across his desk and spoke warningly. "Each of these three men is dangerous. You understand that? Mrs. Carson, the girls say that someone tried to break into your apartment. The intruder may have intended to steal something, but I think it's more likely he meant to frighten or harm you."

Mrs. Carson looked pale and nodded.

Captain Brown continued. "Denver will stand for no interference in his plot against his sister. And if he really is running a car-winning racket, and thinks you're trying to spoil it, he will play very rough indeed. I want you to keep your doors locked at all times and stay alert. That goes for all of you."

They promised to do as the captain said.

"Meanwhile, we will keep unobtrusive watch on Mrs. Campbell's shop," he said, "and I will put out tracers on Denver and his accomplices. I'll check wax museums to see if he has tried to dispose of the stolen property."

"We may have a lead on him," Jean said, "in Oak Falls. If we're right, we'll call you."

Then the girls and Mrs. Carson walked the Queen home. Before they left her apartment, she said, "I do feel better now, and all the thanks go to you three."

On the way uptown in the taxi, Jean said, "What I don't understand is why Denver sent the bearded man to our apartment the first day we came to New York. How could he have known then that we were interested in his lucky-number racket, or that we would be working on the Wax Queen's mysteries?"

No one had an answer.

"Right now I'm so hungry, I couldn't figure out what two and two is," Louise said with a grin.

Mrs. Carson clapped a hand to her head. "Oh, of course!" she exclaimed. "How could I have forgotten? You poor darlings have had no supper!"

She stopped the taxi two blocks from their apartment house and took the girls into a small, candlelighted Italian restaurant.

An hour later the Danas sat back and sighed. "Now I feel better!" said Jean. "I could tackle anything. Just lead me to it!"

In good spirits the three walked home, and were still talking lightheartedly when Cousin Cynthia unlocked the front door to her apartment.

"Oh," she said, "it's stuffy in here. Let's open the windows right away. I locked them all before we left!"

Louise cut across the dark dining room and entered the kitchen.

A cool breeze brushed her face. The window was wide open!

CHAPTER XIII

Lucky Number

LOUISE stared at the open window, her heart pounding. Someone had entered the apartment! Was the intruder still there, hiding somewhere in the dark rooms?

"I must warn Jean and Cousin Cynthia," she thought. But before she could move, a scream rang out.

"Cousin Cynthia!" Louise dashed back through the dining room and into the small hall which led to the bedrooms.

The light was on in Mrs. Carson's room. Jean and her cousin stood in front of the dresser, looking at the mirror. Scrawled across it in red were the words: *Mind Your Own Business!*

"Someone got in again," Jean said shakily.

With a trembling hand, Cousin Cynthia picked up a broken lipstick from a little gold basket of cosmetics. "He used this to write with."

"Let's check our room, Louise," said Jean. "Come on!"

"Wait! Go quietly," Louise said. "Whoever did it might still be here."

Cautiously the three went up the hall. Jean reached into their room and turned on the wall switch. No one there! But printed in red on their mirror was the warning: *Danas, Go Home—Or Else!*

"But how did anyone get in?" asked Cousin Cynthia. "I know I locked all the windows and doors."

"I'll show you," Louise said softly, "but first call the police. It's wisest to let them tackle the intruder—if there is one. Tell them to come to the kitchen door," she went on. "Meanwhile, we'll keep watch. If anyone is here and makes a break for it, we'll try to stop him."

The three thought uneasily of the two dark bedrooms they had not looked into and the several large closets in the old-fashioned apartment. After Mrs. Carson had made a low-voiced call to the police station, Louise led the way to the kitchen and switched on the light. The room was empty. The window was still wide open.

"I know I locked that," Cousin Cynthia said positively.

"Here's the answer," whispered Louise. She pointed to a round, neat hole in the glass above the lock. "The intruder made this hole with a glass cutter, then reached through and unlocked the window."

"But how did he reach the fire escape?" asked Cousin Cynthia. "The bottom is high off the ground."

"I'll go down," said Jean, "and see if I can find out."

"Take this," said Cousin Cynthia, giving her a flashlight from a cabinet drawer.

"Thanks. Keep your eyes and ears open," Jean cautioned as she climbed over the windowsill.

Jean made her way quietly down the old fire escape. Here and there a light shone out on the metal steps, but at the second floor, where they ended, it was dark.

The young detective beamed her flashlight into the narrow alley below. A cat streaked out from behind a barrel and disappeared into the blackness. But nothing else stirred. Jean played the light along the edge of the fire escape.

Suddenly she spotted a tiny strand of something caught on the rusty metal. She picked it up and examined it carefully. A shred of rope! "So that's how he did it!" Jean thought.

She hastened up the iron stairs, climbed back inside, and showed her find.

"The intruder threw a rope over the movable part of the fire escape and pulled it down," she said.

"After he climbed up, the bottom rose again. All he had to do was detach his rope and come up. To reach the ground again, he only needed to go down the stairs. The bottom of the fire escape tilted downward under his weight."

"I hope he has already gone," Louise whispered.

As she spoke, there was a knock on the hall door behind the curtain. Louise opened it and admitted two policemen.

Swiftly they searched the apartment, but the intruder was gone. "That's a relief!" said Cousin Cynthia.

After one of the officers had jotted down the facts in his report book, Louise asked if they would inform Captain Brown what had happened. "He's in a different precinct, I know," she added, "but this incident is connected with a case he is working on."

The policemen promised and left.

"Now what'll we do about that broken window?" Cousin Cynthia asked with a sigh.

As she spoke, the telephone rang. Louise went to the hall to answer. It was Aunt Harriet calling to see if the girls still intended to come home the next day.

"Yes," said Louise, and suggested that they bring Cousin Cynthia with them.

Aunt Harriet agreed at once. "I'm sorry, dear," she added, "but I couldn't find out if Mr. Denver is in charge of the drawing for the car. I haven't been able to get in touch with Mr. Welsh, the carnival chairman."

"Never mind," said Louise. "We'll find out tomorrow."

When she returned to the kitchen to report the conversation, a strange sight met her eyes. In front of the window was a table and piled on it were two chairs with a small stool on top of them, and crowning it all, a stack of pots and pans.

"Cousin Cynthia and I have prepared a reception for our caller," Jean said with a grin. "At least we'll hear him if he tries to get in again."

But the night passed quietly and in the morning the precarious tower was still in place.

The girls had persuaded their cousin to go to Oak Falls with them. While she was packing, Louise and Jean went to the Wax Queen's shop. When Osmo let them in, he quickly assured them that the sculptress was all right, despite her harrowing evening. He said that he had been greatly shocked when he learned what had happened, but felt that with the police keeping close watch on the place, no one would try to force his way in.

"I hope you're right," said Louise, and asked where the Wax Queen was.

"In her studio. She's making another bust."

"We came to say good-by," Jean told the elderly man. "We're going home."

Osmo looked worried. "I'm very sorry to hear that. I admit to feeling safer when you're around."

He seemed so genuinely affected by their leave-taking that they quickly assured him they would be back soon.

The Wax Queen had heard them arrive and came out now to greet them affectionately. "We hope to locate your brother tonight," said Jean, and explained they were flying to Oak Falls that afternoon. The Queen looked worried and begged them to be careful.

Before leaving, the girls looked over the figures that were for sale and decided to buy a black wax cat for Aunt Harriet. As soon as it was wrapped they said good-by, then took a bus back to the apartment.

A new pane of glass had been put in the window and lunch was ready.

At two o'clock the girls and their cousin set off for the airport. The plane took off exactly on time, and Miss Dana was at the Oak Falls airport to meet them.

"I'm so happy you came," she said. "It was getting kind of lonesome here."

"Even with Applecore around?" Jean asked.

"Applecore? What's that?" Cousin Cynthia questioned.

Aunt Harriet laughed. "That's Louise and Jean's nickname for the young woman who works for us. Her name is Cora Appel."

Jean laughed. "Applecore is good-natured and

helpful, but oh, is she clumsy! She's always falling or knocking something over, but she's fun, anyway."

Miss Dana said she was to pick up the girl at a supermarket. She drove directly there and they waited in front.

"Here comes Applecore," Louise told her cousin.

A frowzy-looking girl in a flapping coat was hurrying toward them. They were surprised that she did not have her packages in a cart. Instead, she was clutching two huge bags, one in each arm.

Louise and Jean jumped out to help her. Before they had gone five feet, Applecore tripped. One bag flew from her arm and the contents spilled out on the pavement. Louise and Jean tried not to laugh as they chased the rolling grapefruit and helped her gather up the canned goods.

"I'm terribly sorry," said Cora. "Hi, Louise and Jean. How are you? Don't ask me how I am. I'm as bad as ever."

The girls laughed. "No harm done," said Louise. She introduced Cousin Cynthia and the group drove home.

Half an hour later, the Danas and their visitor were having tea in the living room, while the girls told their aunt all that had happened in New York. As they were talking, Applecore entered with a plate of strawberry tarts, which she began to pass.

"Someone is certainly trying to frighten you off

the case," Miss Dana said to the girls, "but I can't understand how they knew you were in New York."

"Or where you intended to stay," added Cousin Cynthia.

Suddenly Cora gave a loud gasp, stopped short, and the tarts slid to one side of the plate.

Louise leaped to save them. "Take it easy, Applecore!" she said, and set the pastry on the table. "What's the matter?"

The young maid looked stricken. "Oh, no," she said. "How could I?"

"How could you what?" Jean asked.

"I'm terrible. I forgot," Cora said. "Oh, please girls—and Miss Dana—forgive me."

"Cora," Aunt Harriet said kindly, "whatever it is, sit down and tell us." She patted the sofa beside her and Applecore perched miserably on the edge.

"It was this way," she said. "The day you left for New York, Miss Dana, a man called up and asked how he could get in touch with the girls. He said it was an urgent case and I got so excited I told him where you all were going to be."

"Did you ask his name?" queried Jean.

"No, I was too excited," said Cora, shamefaced. "I meant to tell you about it, but the whole thing slipped my mind till I heard you talking."

Miss Dana sighed. "It doesnt' matter now," she said. "Just forget the incident."

"Yes, ma'am," said the maid, and repeated her

apologies again. Dejected, she went back to the kitchen.

"Now we know how we were found," said Louise.

"And I'll bet someone's been keeping track of us ever since," Cousin Cynthia declared.

"Maybe," Jean said, then chuckled. "But tonight we'll be doing the tracking!"

That evening the three Danas and Mrs. Carson went to the carnival.

Immediately the girls sought out the chairman, Mr. Welsh. Louise asked him if Mr. Denver was in charge of the prizes.

When the man said Yes, the girls felt a thrill of excitement.

"But he sent word he couldn't come tonight," Mr. Welsh went on. "He asked me to take care of things."

Louise was stunned. Had Denver found out that the Danas were in Oak Falls and stayed away deliberately?

Jean said to Mr. Welsh, "Do you know where he is?"

The chairman paused a moment. "It seems to me that I recall seeing a schedule which said he was to appear two nights from now at a carnival in a place called Harper. That's outside New York City."

"Thank you very much," said Louise, and hurried back to her family. Quickly she explained what had happened and said, "I think we should report this to Captain Brown right away."

The others agreed. Aunt Harriet said, "Why don't you girls go home and make the call? Cynthia and I will remain here." She smiled. "It's just possible we may win a prize!"

"Hope you do," said Jean.

The sisters hurried away. When they reached the house, Louise put in the call.

Captain Brown was interested in their news. "I'll want you and your sister to go to that Harper carnival with a couple of detectives. Get a good look at whoever draws the number and wins. If you're sure they're the same two girls you saw at Penfield and in New Jersey, we'll arrest them and Denver."

Louise and Jean were elated. "He's practically in our grasp!" exclaimed Jean as Louise put down the phone. "Once the police have him for the car racket, he won't be able to threaten his sister any more!"

"I hope you're right," said Louise. "I can hardly wait till Thursday night."

Presently the girls heard the car come into the driveway and a few minutes later their cousin and aunt walked in. Miss Dana was carrying a small, good-looking clock radio.

She beamed. "I won this! My lucky number was the first one drawn out of the hat!"

"Congratulations!" the sisters said together.

"It's a wonderful radio," said Miss Dana. "It has a timer so you can set the radio to go on and off whenever you want to."

Cousin Cynthia spoke up. "You can put it alongside your bed and fall asleep to music."

Louise said, "I'll bet you'll be the first one to bed tonight."

Her aunt said she was going immediately and asked them all to come up and hear the radio. Lights were extinguished and the group went upstairs.

The girls gave Aunt Harriet the wax cat they had bought for her. She was delighted and placed it proudly on her bedside table.

When Louise and Jean awakened the next morning, Aunt Harriet's new radio was on. They went in to speak to her and she said she was trying out the alarm. It was set for 10 A.M. to remind her of an appointment she had with the dentist.

Just before ten o'clock, the girls again went into the room. Cora was there, using the duster attachment of the vacuum cleaner on the table where the clock radio and the cat stood.

Suddenly the alarm went off. Cora jumped, startled. The vacuum attachment swept across the table and knocked the wax cat to the floor.

"Oh!" Cora screamed as the statue broke into several pieces. Instantly she burst into tears.

Louise and Jean stared at the ruined wax figure. With a sudden gasp, Jean stooped down and picked up one of the pieces.

"Look!" she exclaimed. "A diamond!"

CHAPTER XIV

The Wrong Cat

THE maid looked as if she had been struck dumb. She tried to speak but could not say a word. Aunt Harriet and Cousin Cynthia had come into the bedroom upon hearing Jean's outcry.

"What's this about a diamond?" Aunt Harriet said. "I didn't think I—"

She then saw the broken statue and the diamond in Jean's outstretched hand. "This was inside the cat," Jean said.

"How astonishing!" Cousin Cynthia remarked.

Louise said she wondered why the Wax Queen had hidden it there. "She either forgot the diamond when she sold us the cat or—"

"Or," Jean finished the sentence, "she didn't know it was there."

"If so," Aunt Harriet spoke up, "then who did put the diamond there?" She smiled. "Another unanswered question in the mystery."

Jean said she wished they could communicate with the Wax Queen immediately, but this was out of the question. She had no telephone and they preferred not to discuss such a confidential matter in a telegram.

"Somehow I feel sure this is connected with the other strange events at the Queen's studio," Jean said.

"There's only one thing to do," said Louise. "Go back to New York and try to learn the truth."

"But you just got here," Aunt Harriet objected. "I haven't seen much of you."

The girls hugged her affectionately. "We'll spend every minute with you today and take the night plane back to the city," Louise said.

Her aunt was finally mollified and they all spent a delightful day together. Late in the afternoon Aunt Harriet drove Mrs. Carson and her nieces to the airport. The flight to New York included dinner and it seemed to the girls as if they had hardly finished eating before it was time to get off.

"What a beautiful night it is!" Jean burst out as they drove in the limousine toward the city. Lighted windows in the tall buildings glittered and the traffic hummed along the busy highway.

"Somewhere in that maze is the answer to this new question," Jean went on. "Anybody want to bet with me when we'll solve it?"

"I have a hunch it will be soon," Louise replied.

"The whole case just *has* to be settled before we go back to school."

All this time, Cousin Cynthia had been very quiet. When the girls asked if anything were worrying her, she said:

"I just hope everything will be all right at the apartment. So many things have happened there lately that I'm almost afraid to go in and look."

Louise suggested that after the last episode, the building superintendent would have taken extra precautions. She said, "Cousin Cynthia, please don't worry."

But their cousin was unable to shake off the mood. Trembling, she unlocked the door of the apartment and entered the living room. She did not say a word as they went through the other rooms. Everything looked just the way they had left it.

"I guess I'm unnecessarily jittery," she said. "I'm sorry."

The Danas hugged their cousin and said they did not blame her a bit. Louise added, "Now let's have a cookie and a glass of milk and go to bed."

As they were eating, Mrs. Carson calmed down and presently yawned. Louise winked at Jean and the three went to their rooms.

The girls were up early, eager to return to their sleuthing. Quietly they prepared bacon and eggs and toast, intending to let their cousin sleep. But before long, she appeared at the kitchen door in her robe, smiling drowsily.

"Umm, smells delicious," she said.

"What'll you have?" Jean asked jauntily.

"Everything," Cousin Cynthia said with a smile. "How I do love to be waited on!"

As the three enjoyed their hearty breakfast, the girls saw that Mrs. Carson's usually cheerful spirits had been restored and she was willing to let them go to Greenwich Village alone to pursue their sleuthing.

"It's awfully early, though," Louise said doubtfully. "I'd hate to wake the Wax Queen."

"Don't worry about that," Mrs. Carson said. "She told me that she rises and starts work at dawn every day."

"Good!" said Jean. "We'll be early birds, too."

When the sisters arrived at the shop and rang the bell, Osmo opened the door. A look of utter astonishment crossed his face. "I thought you went away," he said.

Jean chuckled. "We did, but one can travel fast in a plane. Osmo, aren't you glad to see us?" she teased.

"I am indeed glad," he said, in a most hospitable tone.

"Thank you," said Louise. "We have a great surprise for the Wax Queen. Is she here?"

Osmo nodded. "She's in her studio. I've never seen her working more intently. The Queen must be making something very special."

"May we go in?" Jean asked.

"Yes."

As the girls stood in the doorway of the studio, the sculptress looked up.

"My dears!" she exclaimed. "I am very happy to see you, but you caught me with my surprise!"

She pointed to the wax figure on which she was working. It was Jean!

"Oh, Mrs. Campbell!" Jean exclaimed. "You're marvelous to do this." She gave the woman a hug. "It looks just like me."

"It certainly does," Louise agreed. "It's perfectly lovely."

The Queen seemed pleased and murmured her thanks. Then she gazed at the girls shrewdly. "You have come because something has happened which you need to ask me about."

Louise admitted that the sculptress was right.

"Don't tell me!" the Wax Queen said. "I'll tell you. I have had a vision of what took place."

The woman smiled. "The wax cat you bought from me to take to your aunt was knocked off a table and smashed."

Louise and Jean looked at each other, utterly astonished. This woman truly was psychic!

"You have told us exactly what happened," Louise said. "What else did you see?"

"That was all."

Osmo spoke up. "Was the cat smashed to pieces?"

"I'm afraid so," said Louise.

"Dear me, that's too bad," said the elderly man and chuckled.

The Queen smiled. "Don't mind Osmo, girls. He has an odd sense of humor. Please go on with what you were saying."

"We have a surprise for you," Louise went on. From her purse she brought out the diamond which had been found in the broken cat. "Can you tell us anything about this?"

"Why, no. Where did it come from?"

"The black wax cat we bought from you," Louise replied. "If you didn't put it inside when you were molding the figure, then somebody else did."

All this time Louise and Jean had been observing the Wax Queen for any sign of guilt. But she displayed none. Instead, she clapped her hands to her head and rushed out to the shelf in the shop, calling to the girls, "Follow me!"

When they reached the outer room, the sculptress turned pale. "Oh, you bought the wrong cat!" she wailed.

Jean spoke up. "What do you mean?"

The Queen explained that there had been two black wax cats that looked very similar. One of them she had molded herself. The other had been damaged and brought into the shop by a young woman who asked the Wax Queen to repair it.

"That diamond must belong to her," the sculptress said. "But why in the world was it inside the cat?"

"You caught me with my surprise!" the sculptress
exclaimed

Louise said with a sigh, "It's one more mystery."

The sculptress looked worried. "What will I tell the young lady when she comes? She'll be here this afternoon. It will not only be embarrassing to tell her the cat is smashed, but what will we do about the diamond? Perhaps it was stolen or smuggled."

"Maybe she doesn't know anything about it," Louise remarked.

"What's her name?" Jean asked.

"Dora Bushwick."

Louise suggested that the Wax Queen keep the jewel in a safe place until they found out if it was the customer's property.

"All right," said the woman. She took the diamond from Louise, wrapped it in a clean tissue, and put it in her smock pocket. "I'll take it upstairs later."

Suddenly the Wax Queen dropped into a chair. She had turned very pale and the girls were afraid she was about to faint.

"I—I need food," she said weakly. "I forgot to eat breakfast. A little nourishment will give me strength so I can quickly make a new wax cat for Miss Bushwick."

"Why can't you offer her the one up there on the shelf?" Jean inquired.

The Queen shook her head. "It is not exactly

like the one Miss Bushwick brought here. I must duplicate her cat as quickly as possible."

She gave her apartment keys to Louise, and the girls hurried off. The sculptress called after them, "Bring food for all of us."

Louise unlocked the street door and the girls ascended the stairway. With the second key, they let themselves into the apartment. The blinds were drawn and the living room was dim. The next instant, the girls froze in their tracks.

Mr. Denver was seated in a chair!

CHAPTER XV

The Spook

"Oh!" Jean cried out. "We didn't know anybody was here!"

Mr. Denver stared straight at the sisters. He did not rise from the chair and, in fact, did not move.

Suddenly Louise dashed forward and burst into laughter. "Jean, this is only a wax statue!"

Both girls felt sheepish. Nevertheless, they were amazed at Mrs. Campbell. They assumed she had made the wax figure, but if she disliked her brother so intensely, why had she done this?

The girls stared at "Mr. Denver" a few minutes. Then Jean pretended to shake hands with him. "Howdy, Mr. Spook?" she said. "What's inside that little old brain of yours? Tell me your secrets and I'll give you a nice, new shiny automobile."

Louise giggled. "Wouldn't it be great if he

could talk? Every time he said something that wasn't true, we'd tell him exactly what we found out."

"You bet!" said Jean. "Old Mr. Spook would find that he had been spooked."

Louise started for the kitchen. "Let's not forget what we came up here to do—get some food for Mrs. Campbell."

Within twenty minutes they had made ham-and-egg-sandwiches for the sculptress, Osmo, and themselves. Cocoa was quickly prepared and the whole meal put on a tray.

"I didn't think I could eat again," said Jean, "but it looks so good, I've changed my mind!"

"I'll carry it," Louise offered.

As she entered the living room, she gave a cry of astonishment. The tray almost fell from her hands and all the food slid to one side. The cocoa spilled onto the saucers and tray.

"What's the matter?" Jean asked, coming through the doorway behind her sister.

Louise was gazing ahead, speechless. Jean looked too. She gasped.

"Mr. Denver" was gone!

Louise set the tray on a table. As she turned back to look at the empty chair, her eyes caught sight of the wax figure. It was now seated on a sofa in the corner of the room. She nodded toward it.

Jean dashed across the room, half expecting that this time Mr. Denver would be real. He was not. It was only the wax statue, which had been fashioned in a sitting position.

"You didn't hear any kind of a noise, did you?" Louise asked Jean.

Her sister shook her head. "If I had, you can bet I would have come to look right away."

"Well, the wax figure couldn't move itself, so somebody *was* in here. We'd better go ask the Wax Queen if she or Osmo came in. That old man moves so quickly, he could have been here without our knowing it."

"But why?" Jean asked.

"I don't know, unless he wanted to scare us. He has an odd sense of humor."

Puzzled, Louise picked up the tray and the girls went down the stairs. On the street they looked right and left, but at the moment it was deserted. They rang the shop bell and Osmo opened the door. He told them that Mrs. Campbell was in the studio and followed them there.

"Oh, that looks good," the Wax Queen said, getting up from her work.

Louise answered, "It's a little sloppy because I got quite a scare while I was carrying it through your apartment."

"Scare?" the woman asked.

Louise told the story. The sculptress and her assistant looked at each other. The Danas thought they saw fear in their eyes.

"We weren't upstairs," Osmo said earnestly. "You say someone moved the statue?"

"Yes." Seeing the concern in his face, both girls were convinced he had not been responsible for the trick.

The Wax Queen explained that a few weeks before, she had felt a great urge to make a wax figure of her brother. "But when the piece was finished, I took a dislike to it and put it in a closet in the apartment. Because of the thefts in my shop, I thought it might be a good idea to use Fred to scare away any thief who might break into the apartment, so this morning I sat him in the chair. I'm sorry the figure frightened you girls. I should have told you it was there."

The woman seemed to have forgotten the crux of the matter—that someone had moved "Mr. Denver." Gently Louise reminded her of the fact.

She frowned. "There might have been a burglar. He could have hidden when you girls came in; and then, while you were in the kitchen, continued his work and made his escape."

Louise suggested that they eat, then go upstairs to see if anything had been stolen.

An hour later Mrs. Campbell reported that nothing was missing and the Danas admitted they had found no clues to the identity of the intruder.

As they all stood in the middle of the living room wondering how to proceed on the mystery, Louise suddenly snapped her fingers. "I have a hunch, Jean. Let's go to the locksmith."

The sculptress and Osmo looked puzzled. "I'll explain later," Louise said with a smile. "There might be nothing to my idea at all."

Jean guessed what her sister was thinking, and when the two girls reached the street, she said, "You believe the intruder went to the locksmith and somehow managed to get duplicate keys to the apartment and perhaps the shop?"

"Yes. And I have a further hunch that the person might be someone the locksmith knows and trusts."

The girls hurried along the street. When they walked into the locksmith's shop, he was standing at his key-making machine, grinding out a duplicate for an order. He was alone in the place and gave the girls a friendly smile.

"You back so soon?" he asked.

Louise interrupted him. "What do you mean? We haven't been here since the night you put in the new locks for the Wax Queen."

The man stared at the sisters in utter astonishment. "You weren't here last evening?"

"No. We weren't even in Greenwich Village."

The locksmith frowned. "I could have sworn you were. You sure? You're not spoofing me?"

Jean spoke up. "What is this? A game? We weren't here."

The man wagged his head. "I guess I've done a

dreadful thing. Did you have some trouble at the shop?"

"Not in the shop, but in the Wax Queen's apartment. An intruder got in there."

The locksmith went ash white. "Here's the story. About seven o'clock last night two girls came in here. They sure looked a lot like you and they gave your names."

"They used our names?" Jean exclaimed.

The man nodded. "They said they were Louise and Jean Dana. Didn't I remember them? They had come to get me to put new locks on the doors of the Wax Queen's shop and apartment. I said yes. Then one of them smiled and said, 'You know how absent-minded the Wax Queen is. She misplaced her keys and wants you to give us the duplicates you have of them.' "

"Please go on," Louise urged as the man paused.

He told them that at the Queen's request he had kept copies of her keys. The girls had showed him a note signed by the sculptress, authorizing him to do what they asked.

"That was a forgery," said Louise.

The man nodded unhappily. "I can see now how those other young ladies look different from you. But I didn't then, so I gave them the keys—for the front and back doors of the apartment as well as the one for the shop.

"What did the girls look like?" Louise asked.

The locksmith gazed into space, then said,

"They were about your size and their hair was the same as yours—one blonde, one brunette." But he could not remember any other details.

He clasped and unclasped his hands nervously. "What was stolen?"

The girls explained briefly, then asked him to come as soon as possible to replace the locks on the doors.

"I'm terribly sorry this happened," the man said. "I'll pick up some special locks and install them tomorrow morning."

As the Danas stepped out onto the street, Jean said, "I'll bet those two girls were Mr. Denver's helpers, wearing wigs. He must have sneaked into the apartment—or they did. But the big question is why."

Before Louise could answer, a tall, square-jawed man in a gray business suit and felt hat stepped out of a neighboring doorway.

"Excuse me," he said quietly, removing his hat. "Are you Louise and Jean Dana?"

The girls were taken aback. "Why—yes," said Louise.

Pulling a badge from his pocket, the man cupped it in his hand so the girls could see it. "You will come with me, please," he said. "I have an important message for you from Captain Brown."

CHAPTER XVI

A Disappointing Chase

THE stranger indicated the coffee shop next door. "We can talk in there," he said.

The girls glanced again at the detective badge in his hand. "All right," said Louise.

The man led the way to the coffee shop and opened the door for them. Inside, he chose a table by the window. The proprietor nodded at his greeting, but continued wiping the counter.

The stranger took identification from his pocket and placed it before the girls. "My name is James Murphy," he said as they examined the papers. "I'm one of the detectives who is watching the wax shop."

Satisfied, Louise handed back the identification. "You say you have a message for us from Captain Brown?"

"Yes. He tried to reach you at Mrs. Carson's and she informed him you were with Mrs. Campbell. When I went there, the old man told me you had gone to the locksmith." The detective hitched his chair closer to the table and lowered his voice. "The message is about the carnival at Harper tonight."

"We're all ready," Jean said impetuously. "Denver has been up to some more of his tricks, and the sooner we catch him the better."

Louise smiled. "We can hardly wait to go."

The man's face was grim. "The trip is off," he said flatly.

The girls stared for a moment. "Off?" Jean said in a tone of disbelief.

The man nodded.

"But why?" Louise asked. "That's the only lead we have on Denver. It's a chance to see whether—"

"He won't be there," the detective interrupted. "The carnival chairman informed Harper police that Denver has backed out on the job." He added that the police were trying to trace the showman, but he seemed to have vanished into thin air.

Bitter disappointment showed in the girls' faces.

"He ducked out on the Oak Falls carnival, too," Louise said. "I'm afraid he knows we're on to him."

"Yes. That's what we think," said Detective Murphy. "And Captain Brown is worried about you. He's afraid Denver will try to get you out of the picture. He warns you to be especially careful from here on."

"All right, we will," said Jean.

"Can you tell us where your stake-out post is?" Jean asked as the detective stood up to go.

The man smiled slightly. "We watch from the attic window of the tall, narrow house across the street from the shop."

"The one over the French bakery?" Louise asked.

"Yes." Then he added, "We have radio contact with the precinct, of course. A man is stationed on the next street in a house which overlooks the back yard of the Wax Queen's place."

"Have you seen anyone except Mrs. Campbell go into the apartment since last evening?" Jean asked.

"No. Why?"

"There have been developments in the case," Louise said.

"Report them to Captain Brown, then," the detective said. He excused himself and left.

The girls decided to stop at the shop to tell the Wax Queen what they had discovered, then go on to the police station.

As they left the coffee shop, Louise said to Jean, "It's obvious that the Wax Queen's brother is trying to get her to move. He is not only stealing some of her work, but now he's trying to make her apartment spooky so she'll be too frightened to stay. If he hadn't found the figure of himself, he'd have used some other trick to scare her."

"I think you're right," said Jean. "He probably figures if he can break her spirit and scare her out of her home and shop, she'll be glad to sell the business cheap."

"It's a heartless scheme," said Louise.

"Do you think Denver himself was in the apartment and moved the statue?" Jean asked.

Louise shrugged. "Yes, or it could have been either of those girls. After all, they're the ones who have the keys."

As the sisters neared the shop, they saw a customer entering—a young woman attractively dressed and wearing a large fashionable hat. They saw only her back and wondered who she might be.

When they reached the door, it was opened by Osmo. He put his finger to his lips as they entered.

"That young lady who left the cat is here," he whispered. "The Queen wants to handle the matter of the broken figure herself, but she would like you to listen from upstairs." The girls looked puzzled as the old man beckoned them outside.

"Go up to the kitchen," he said, giving them the keys. "From there you can hear everything that's going on in the Queen's studio. I'm on my way to the grocery," he added, and started down the street.

The Danas hurried up to the apartment. Beside the stove was a hot-air register, and through it came the angry voice of Miss Bushwick from below.

"Smashed! You careless old woman!" she exclaimed.

"I told you I did not drop it. It was sold by mistake because it looked very much like a figure I had made. I have modeled a new cat for you and I don't think you can tell the difference."

"You don't, don't you?" the young woman cried out angrily. "Well, you're wrong. That cat was extremely valuable."

"Yes, I know," the sculptress said. "But although the figure was well-fashioned, there was another reason why it was valuable."

The Danas could imagine that her bright eyes were boring into those of her caller.

"You make me sick," Miss Bushwick said. "Where are the pieces of the broken cat?"

"Thrown away days ago."

At this, the caller gave a shrill cry. "You idiot!" she exclaimed.

Then there was a silence.

After a few moments the Bushwick girl said in a low and threatening voice, "I don't believe you. I think you're holding out on me, and I'm going to find out!"

"Don't come any closer!" cried Mrs. Campbell.

The next second the sisters heard the Queen scream. Had the young woman hit her?

"Come on!" exclaimed Louise. "We'd better get down there!"

The two girls rushed to the street. As they

reached it, the shop door opened and Dora Bushwick dashed out. The Danas recognized her as Denver's red-haired accomplice at the Penfield carnival!

"Catch her!" cried Louise.

Jean, in the lead, made a dive for the young woman and caught her by the wrist. With a cry of pain, the girl opened her fist. Something dropped from it.

The diamond!

As Jean and Louise looked at the ground, Dora Bushwick pulled herself free and ran down the street. Jean picked up the diamond, then joined her sister in pursuing the red-haired girl.

The few seconds' delay gave Dora Bushwick a head start. At the curb stood a car with the motor running and the door open. She jumped in and the automobile sped off as the door slammed shut. Louise had been inches from her!

Though frustrated at the near catch, the Danas had the presence of mind to memorize the license number, which had been issued in New York State.

"So Dora Bushwick is the redhead, Dolores Doremus!" said Louise.

"Yes, and that girl at the wheel was the other one who helps Mr. Denver at the car drawings."

As Louise and Jean hurried back to the shop, they realized that the officers on watch must have seen and reported the chase. At the door Louise said, "I'll check on the Queen. You'd better take the diamond to Captain Brown and tell him everything that has happened."

Jean hurried to the police station, where she immediately gave the captain the license number of the suspect's car.

"We've sent out an alarm," he said, "but we didn't have the car license." He reached for a telephone and added the number to his earlier instructions. When he turned back to Jean, the captain said, "Thank you for reporting this so promptly. We have an excellent chance to pick them up now."

"And they can give us a lead to Denver," Jean added hopefully. Then she told him all the latest developments in the case.

The captain frowned. "But how did the intruder get into the apartment? The stake-out men report no strangers going in the front. They've been given descriptions of you and your sister," he explained. "The alley next to the building leads to the back yard where there's an outside staircase going up to the apartment. The men on duty in the front and rear say you were the only ones to go in and out that way."

Jean looked amazed. "But we didn't!" Then, at once, she understood. "I'll bet it was Denver's two girls. They were wearing wigs again."

"I see," said the captain. "The detective made the same mistake the locksmith did."

Jean nodded. "But where does the diamond fit in?"

"That's one of the questions we'll ask those young ladies when we catch them," the captain said.

"In the meantime," said Jean, "I'd better leave the diamond with you for safekeeping."

After giving it to the captain, Jean returned to the Wax Queen's shop. Osmo opened the door. He was trembling with fright.

"What's the matter?" Jean asked.

In a feeble voice and wringing his hands, Osmo said, "Something terrible has happened to the Queen!"

CHAPTER XVII

Black Magic

FEARFUL of what had happened to the sculptress, Jean ran to the studio. The Queen lay on the floor, covered with a crocheted afghan. She was unconscious.

Beside her knelt a doctor who was treating a cut on the back of her head, while Louise watched anxiously. Seeing Jean, she stepped over and quietly told about finding the woman unconscious.

"I guess the Bushwick girl knocked her down. In falling, the Queen must have struck her head on something sharp—probably the corner of the stand she uses for her sculpturing."

As Jean looked worriedly at the woman, Louise went on, "Osmo was too shaken to do anything, so I covered her and ran to the drugstore to call a doctor. He hasn't been here very long."

A few moments later the physician closed his black bag and stood up. Louise introduced him as

Dr. Butler. He wrote out a prescription and asked if the Danas intended to stay with Mrs. Campbell.

Before they had a chance to answer, the Wax Queen opened her eyes. After a few seconds she endeavored to get up.

Staring at the doctor, she said, "Who are you? And what happened to me? Oh, yes, I remember. The diamond!" she cried wildly. "It's gone! That dreadful young woman stole it!"

Louise took hold of the sculptress' hands and said gently, "You were knocked out. Jean and I took the diamond away from Dora Bushwick. The police have it now."

"Thank goodness." A look of relief came over the Wax Queen's face. "Thank you," she murmured. "I was holding the diamond in my hand inside my smock pocket. The girl must have suspected, because she suddenly jerked my hand out and pried it open. Then she grabbed the diamond and knocked me down. Doctor," she added, "I want to get up. I feel all right now."

He helped the Queen to her feet and onto a chair, then said that she must stay in bed until the next morning. When the doctor learned that she lived upstairs, he suggested that she be carried there. "You've had a bad shock," he said.

"I'll sleep right here," the sculptress said. "See that big chest in the wax room? It converts into a bed. I'll stay there."

Dr. Butler nodded. He asked if one of the girls

would pick up some medication in about ten minutes. On the way back to his office, he would leave the prescription at the drugstore on the next block.

"I'll be glad to," said Jean.

When the physician left, the girls went at once to the big chest and raised the lid. Underneath was a thick mattress.

"We'll go up to your apartment and get some sheets and blankets and a pillow," Louise offered.

"They are in the wardrobe in my bedroom," the Queen said weakly.

Osmo gave the girls the keys to the apartment. He stayed with the Wax Queen while they hastened upstairs.

As Louise and Jean stepped into the dim living room, they glanced quickly toward the sofa where "Mr. Denver" had been sitting. He was still there, staring straight ahead.

Jean gave a little giggle of relief. "This place gives me the creeps," she said.

"Mrs. Campbell likes the blinds down, I guess," said Louise, "but it certainly makes the place spooky."

The girls crossed the dining room and stepped into a tiny hall which led to the bedroom.

Suddenly Louise stopped short and gripped her sister's arm. "Listen," she whispered.

The girls stood still in the darkness, straining their ears. Silence.

"I thought I heard a tinkle of glass," Louise whispered, "but maybe I imagined it."

The door to the Queen's bedroom was ajar. The girls pushed it open and entered. Earlier, when they had helped Mrs. Campbell search the apartment, they had been amazed by the unusual bedroom furnishings. There was an enormous canopied bed with brocade side curtains, which were closed. Against one wall was a dressing table with a tall ornate mirror. Next to it stood a heavy carved wardrobe.

As Jean opened it to take out the linens, Louise's eye fell upon an array of fancy perfume bottles on the dresser. One of them was lying on its side! Was this the tinkle of glass she had heard? Who had knocked the perfume bottle over?

Turning her head to warn her sister, Louise glanced into the mirror. She stifled a gasp. Reflected in it were the bed curtains. They were stirring!

Silently she got Jean's attention and pointed to the mirror. Both girls stared, hearts pounding, at the moving brocade.

Suddenly Louise took a deep breath, strode to the bed, and jerked the curtains open.

A sharp hiss sounded and the girls jumped back, startled. There was Caesar, the cat, arching his back and glaring at them!

The Danas collapsed into laughter. Finally they went back to the wardrobe. When they had taken out sheets and a blanket, Jean returned to the bed.

"Sorry, Caesar old boy," she said, picking up a pillow. "We won't disturb you any more."

"He's the one who ought to apologize," said Louise. "He knocked over a perfume bottle and scared me out of a year's growth."

When the girls reached the wax room, they started toward the chest to make up the bed.

"Wait!" the Queen said. "You girls have been very kind. As a reward, I will show you my great secret. Help me to the bed."

They obeyed. Then the sculptress lifted up one side of the mattress and told the girls to look below it. Revealed was a marvelous collection of wax dolls arranged side by side in a long tray.

"They're exquisite!" Jean exclaimed. "Did you make these?"

"Oh, no," the sculptress responded. "They date back many centuries. I have been collecting them for years. These represent famous kings and queens of long ago."

She pointed out Mary Queen of Scots, Empress Eugenie of France, and Queen Isabella of Spain. "They are the loveliest, I think."

Warming to her subject, Mrs. Campbell told the girls that the art of portraiture in waxes was older than the art of painting. "In the fifteenth century busts of noble gentlemen and ladies were often carved in relief on small wax medallions. Sometimes their portraits were completed with human hair and the elegance of their costumes by precious stones, tinsel, velvet or scraps of lace."

Louise interrupted gently to say that she would like to hear more about it later. Right now she felt that the Wax Queen should get to bed and rest. As the woman nodded and started to lower the mattress, one end of it came off the angle iron and began to drop toward the wax dolls.

"Oh!" she cried out. Instantly Louise and Jean grabbed the mattress and held it up. The Wax Queen gave a deep sigh as they lowered it into proper position on the angle irons. The Danas then made up the bed.

"Don't you think," Louise said, "that this is a bad place to keep your dolls?"

The sculptress answered that she hid them there so they would be safe from prying eyes. "This is one thing my brother doesn't know about."

After they had settled her comfortably in the bed, Louise went up to the apartment to bring a small bell for the Queen to use in summoning Osmo. Meanwhile, Jean hurried to the drugstore to pick up the prescription.

When the Wax Queen had taken the medicine, she said, "Now tell me what you learned at the locksmith."

Jean related what had happened. The woman nodded thoughtfully. "It slipped my mind this morning that the locksmith had duplicate keys.

But my brother knew it. He was here one day when I had misplaced my previous set of keys. He heard me sending Osmo to borrow the copies."

"Then when he wanted to get into your apartment all he had to do was send his two helpers for the duplicates," Louise remarked.

"You think he ordered those girls to do something at the apartment to frighten me?" the Queen asked.

"Yes," said Jean, and told what she had learned at the police station. "The girls must have been hiding in the living room when Louise and I came in. The figure of Mr. Denver provided a good way to scare us—and you, of course."

A thought came to Louise. She asked the sculptress, "Does your brother have a family?"

The Wax Queen frowned. "Why do you ask?"

Louise smiled. "One of my hunches, I guess. I wonder if those two girls who help him at carnivals are related to him."

"They might be. My brother has two stepdaughters. I have never seen them. My twin and I didn't like his wife, so we've never visited."

"You know," Louise said, "I think we ought to call on your sister. She might have some information which would be useful in solving the mystery."

"We'd have gone sooner," said Jean, "but so much has been happening, there's been no time."

"You should go, of course," the sculptress replied. She gave them her sister's unlisted telephone number and her address. "Tell her to come and see me. There are several things I would like to talk over with her."

The Danas were about to leave when the Wax Queen said, "Don't go yet, but wait in the shop. I feel as if I were about to receive a message. It might have something to do with you. I'll call you when I'm ready."

She closed her eyes and the Danas tiptoed from the room. While waiting, they looked over the fine wax pieces on the shelves in the shop. Both girls suddenly realized that there was one figure which they had not noticed before. Had the sculptress just put it there?

As they gazed at it longer, the wax statue began to look familiar. Jean whispered excitedly, "That's the Egyptian Queen, Nefertiti! But before she was olive-skinned!"

Louise bent forward to look at the name carved on the piece. Yes, it was Queen Nefertiti. But now the statue was white!

The sisters looked at each other, completely baffled. Along with all the other mysteries in this place was there black magic too?

CHAPTER XVIII

Subway Escape

"I wonder if dark-colored wax turns white after a while," said Jean.

"I think not," Louise replied. "If you put beeswax in the sun it'll bleach, but in this dim room I shouldn't think anything would happen."

The Danas decided that for some reason known only to the sculptress, she had whitened the statue of Queen Nefertiti. "When we have a chance, let's ask her. I wonder how long it will be before she calls us back."

Her sister chuckled. "She may fall asleep due to that medicine and we'll have a long wait!"

Just then, however, Mrs. Campbell tinkled the bell which the girls had left with her and they walked quietly into the big room.

Looking up at them, the Wax Queen smiled. "I'm beginning to think that you girls have ESP, too."

"*We* have?" Louise asked, surprised. "How do you figure that?"

She told them that only a little while before, they had inquired about her twin, Winnie. "Now comes a message that something is about to happen to her."

"You mean your brother may harm her?" Jean inquired.

The sculptress explained that she had seen no mental images. She just heard a voice warning her that very soon something would happen to Winnie.

"Please go to her at once," the Wax Queen pleaded. "Maybe you can keep her from being harmed."

"I hope she'll be at home."

"Oh, I forgot to tell you," Mrs. Campbell said. "Sometimes Winnie works part-time in a Mexican gift shop in Rockefeller Center Arcade. If she's not at home, try her at the shop. Go into the uptown Fifth Avenue entrance, then downstairs. When you get to the arcade, keep to the left. I don't remember the name of the place, but I'm sure you'll find it. And one thing more," the Wax Queen added. Her voice was beginning to sound sleepy. "The sealed envelope I gave you—open it today."

The girls promised to do so, said good-by, and left.

"The sealed envelope!" exclaimed Jean. "That means we're in for another surprise today."

"Yes, but it's supposed to be a nice one," Louise reminded her.

The girls walked to the drugstore where Jean went into a public-telephone booth and dialed the number the Wax Queen had given them. The phone rang and rang, but there was no answer.

"I guess we'll have to try the Mexican gift shop," she decided. "But first let's have a bite of lunch at the counter here."

Louise chuckled. "We've had a busy morning, all right. Good thing we had two breakfasts."

After a sandwich and an ice-cream soda, the Danas took a taxi to the Fifth Avenue side of the Rockefeller Center group of buildings.

As they stepped from the cab, Louise looked down the long garden and promenade which lay between two buildings and said, "Aren't those spring flowers gorgeous?"

"And the sun is so warm I'd like to sit down on one of these benches and get a little suntan," Jean remarked. "But I guess we'll have to keep going."

The girls entered the building to their right. As they started for the stairs which led to the lower level, Jean gave a start, then tugged at her sister's arm.

"Look!" she whispered. "That man who just passed us! Isn't he Denver?"

Louise turned quickly. He was hurrying down the corridor. She agreed that it certainly looked like him. "Let's catch up to him!" she suggested.

The girls strode after the man at a brisk pace. Whether he sensed pursuit or had some other reason for looking back over his shoulder, the girls did not know. But when they saw his face they were sure who he was.

Apparently he recognized them, and did not intend to let them overtake him. He began to run, jostling people who were in his way.

The sisters threaded their way among the throng. Denver reached the rear door and darted out into the area of wide walks which ran around each side of a large depressed skating rink.

The fleeing man turned left, dashed to the side street, and ran all the way to the Avenue of the Americas. With the girls close on his heels, he raced down the steps to a subway station. Pulling a token from his pocket, he quickly put it in the slot and went through the turnstile. A train had just pulled into the station and he jumped aboard.

The Danas were stymied. By the time they bought tokens, the train had pulled out and Denver was gone!

Jean was disgusted. "To think we were so close to catching him!"

Louise sighed. "We missed our man, but maybe we saved Miss Winnie Moffat from harm. Perhaps the Wax Queen's ESP warning was about him."

The suspect ran, jostling people who were in his way

The sisters climbed the stairs and walked back to the building where the gift shop was located. They found it easily and inquired for Miss Moffat. When she came from a rear room, they knew at once she was Wendy Moffat Campbell's twin.

The Danas introduced themselves and said they were friends of Mrs. Campbell.

Miss Moffat looked surprised. "You're the Dana girls from Starhurst School?" she asked in complete astonishment.

Jean laughed. "The same."

"I have been meaning to write and thank you for your note," the woman said. "Unfortunately, I do not need to find my brother now. He has found *me* and threatens to do me harm if I do not give him more money."

The girls looked sympathetic. "We saw you at Penfield," Louise said, "and we'd like to know why you tried to stop the drawing."

Fire danced in Miss Moffat's eyes. "I'm sorry to have to tell you that my brother is not honest. I kept hearing of shady deals he pulled, but I could never find him because he uses several aliases. Just by accident, I happened to see him at that carnival. I was visiting a friend who took me there.

"I went to the tent before the drawing, and begged him in tears to give me back the money he had borrowed. He refused and threatened me. I guess I lost my head and tried to stop the drawing.

I was sure it was dishonest, but of course I could prove nothing."

"It's too bad that you didn't succeed," Louise told her, "because we are strongly suspicious that Mr. Denver is running a racket. Did you recognize the girl who was about to draw the number?"

"No," Miss Moffat replied. "Did you?"

The Danas told her of their suspicions, based on what the Wax Queen had told them. They also revealed that the two girls who helped Denver were in town and that one of them had been to the shop and injured Mrs. Campbell. "Your sister would like you to visit her," Louise said.

"Of course I'll go," Miss Moffat answered.

She explained to the shop owner what had happened and went for her coat. She walked out with Louise and Jean.

On the way to Fifth Avenue, Jean said, "What I can't understand is how your brother learned that we were interested in this case."

Winnie Moffat looked troubled. "I'm sorry, but I'm afraid that was my fault. Two days after the Penfield carnival he appeared at my apartment and again threatened me. I told him I was going to hound him until he paid what he owed. I said I had put two clever detectives on his trail and told him who you were."

"That explains it," said Louise. "All he had to do was call our house and the maid told him when and where we'd be in New York."

Jean asked Miss Moffat if she had ever heard that either of the stepdaughters owned a diamond.

"No, I never did," Miss Moffat replied.

"I've been wondering," said Louise, "why you asked us to write to General Delivery instead of your address."

The woman looked bitter. "I was taking no chances. It would not surprise me if Fred kept watch on my mail. The apartment building where I live is old. It would be easy for him to get into my mailbox."

Just then the trio reached the avenue and Miss Moffat's bus came. The Danas helped her aboard and waved good-by.

"Now let's go home," Louise said as the bus rolled off. "Maybe that's where our surprise is."

Jean said, "I almost forgot about the sealed envelope."

Wondering about the surprise, the sisters returned to their cousin's apartment. When they knocked on the door, it was opened by a young man.

"Ken!" exclaimed Louise. "This is marvelous! When did you get here?" Before he could answer, another young man poked his head over Ken's shoulder. "Chris!" Jean exclaimed happily. "What a wonderful surprise!"

After the girls had entered the apartment, the boys told them that they had just arrived in New York.

Cousin Cynthia came forward. "I was so afraid you girls might get tied up with your mystery and not show up here."

Louise chuckled. "Maybe our ESP was working and brought us home."

Jean exclaimed, "The sealed envelope! Let's open it! I'll bet the boys are our surprise."

"I'll get the envelope," Cousin Cynthia said eagerly, "and we'll see!"

While she was gone, Louise and Jean told their visitors about the psychic message. When Mrs. Carson returned, Louise opened the envelope and read the paper inside.

"Jean was right!" she told the others. "The Queen foretold that Chris and Ken would come today!"

"That's a neat trick," said Ken, raising his eyebrows. "How does she do it?"

Jean smiled. "Who knows?" The girls then told the boys all about the case. They finished by relating the day's adventures.

When Cousin Cynthia heard that the Queen had been injured, she was appalled. "You had better go back and see how the poor woman is."

Louise agreed. "How would you like to meet the Wax Queen?" she asked the boys.

"Great!" Chris answered. "I'd like to see those statues of you girls that she made."

"Shall I expect you for dinner?" Cousin Cynthia asked.

Ken laughed. "Better not, Mrs. Carson. We plan to take the girls out to dinner."

"If they're good," Chris added with a twinkle.

The two couples set off. Twenty minutes later Louise was ringing the bell of the shop door. There was no answer! Louise rang again and again. Finally she tried the door. To her surprise, it opened. Had Osmo forgotten to lock it after she and Jean left?

The young people stepped cautiously into the dim shop.

Osmo was standing transfixed before the shelves of statues. His hands were tightly clasped before him and he was staring at the wax figures.

Jean spoke to him gently. "Osmo, what is the matter?"

He whirled, startled. His eyes were wild as he tried to speak. At last he stuttered:

"The—the curse has worked!"

CHAPTER XIX

Chemistry Clue

"WHAT curse?" Jean asked Osmo.

He pointed to the statue of Queen Nefertiti. "She—she has turned white!" he stuttered.

Louise said the girls had noticed this just before they had left that morning. "But what does this have to do with a curse?" she asked.

The elderly man, who was pale as a ghost, explained, "This figure has been in the Moffat family for three generations. The story is that if it should turn white, a curse would fall on the holder."

"You mean," said Jean, "that it has fallen on the Wax Queen?"

"Yes."

The girls realized that the old man was too badly shaken to answer more questions. Louise introduced Ken and Chris, who had been looking around at the various busts and small statues on the shelves.

Osmo shook hands with them, but he seemed to do so automatically. The girls wondered if he fully comprehended that they were there.

"It was such a shock," he said vaguely.

"Where is the Wax Queen now?" Louise inquired gently.

Osmo jerked his thumb toward the rear. "Still resting. Her sister's with her. Both of them are pretty upset."

"We'd like to see them if we may," Jean said.

Osmo said he would find out how the sculptress was feeling. While he was gone, Ken said, "You certainly brought us into the middle of a real mystery!"

"You sure did," Chris added. "This is a spooky old place."

Presently Osmo returned and said the two women would like to see all four callers. As the boys walked in, they glanced around at the wax-melting equipment and up at the huge skylight.

Louise introduced Ken and Chris, and after a few pleasantries, the Wax Queen whispered to Jean, "Could you ask your friends to wait in the shop? I'd like to talk to you girls privately."

Jean suggested that the boys chat with Osmo for a while. They nodded and went off.

"I wanted to talk to you Danas alone because of what has happened. I could hear Osmo telling you the story. It is all true and I am afraid I am the one now who is doomed."

"But, Mrs. Campbell," said Louise, "surely you don't believe in curses being carried out?"

"I'm trying not to," the sculptress answered bravely. "But that, added to something else, has made me feel I am in real danger."

She told the girls that soon after they had left, a messenger had delivered a note signed by her brother. "Again he was proposing that I sell this building and all its contents. The price he named is absolutely ridiculous. Besides, I have told him repeatedly that I do not wish to leave here."

The Wax Queen slid one hand under the covers, brought out a letter, and handed it to the girls. "Read the last four sentences," she said, a slight tremble in her voice.

The note ended:

You had better do as I tell you. The family curse has been put on you. Your days are numbered. Only I can save you.

Winnie Moffat spoke up quietly. "Tradition says that the curse can be lifted, but only by a male member of the family."

Louise and Jean looked at each other, then Jean remarked, "This is just a bluff, Mrs. Campbell. Don't let it scare you."

Louise was staring into space. An idea had suddenly occurred to her. How did Fred Moffat know that the family curse had been put on Mrs.

Campbell? It must mean he knew the statue of Egyptian Queen Nefertiti had turned white!

Louise asked to be excused for a moment. "I want to talk to Ken. He is an excellent chemistry student."

Without further explanation, she left the room and returned to the shop. The two boys were seated, talking with Osmo, but as Louise entered they jumped up.

"Ken," she said, "is there some kind of chemical that could be put on an olive-colored wax statue to turn it white?"

After a few seconds' thought, he replied, "Why yes, sulfur dioxide would do it. Why do you ask?"

Louise was elated. She said, "I believe I have just solved a part of this mystery." Turning to Osmo, she said, "I think Denver came here and whitened the statue to frighten his sister into selling this place."

Osmo's jaw dropped open. "If that is true, you are a fine detective."

Jean had followed Louise into the shop. Hearing her sister's theory, she smiled. "There's someone else who might have poured or sprayed the chemical onto the statue."

"Who?"

"Dora Bushwick," said Jean. "Don't forget she was here."

"She must have been the one," Osmo said. "The

brother did not come, but the young woman was alone in the shop while I announced her to the Queen."

"That reminds me," Louise said. "We haven't checked with the police to see if they located those two girls."

"Suppose Chris and I go to the police station," suggested Jean, "and ask."

The couple left immediately and a short time later were in Captain Brown's office. Good news awaited them.

Dora Bushwick and her companion were in custody!

"That's marvelous!" Jean exclaimed. "Have they confessed yet?"

The captain replied, "No, neither girl will say a word. They had no identification on them, not even drivers' licenses. But we traced the car as the one given to the holder of the lucky number at the New Jersey bazaar."

"We think we know who the girls are," Jean said. "The stepdaughters of Fred Moffat, alias Denver."

Louise informed the captain what she and Jean had learned about the family from the Moffat sisters. She went on to tell about chasing Denver in Rockefeller Center.

"You've done a good job," the captain said. "Knowing who the girls are may help us in getting them to talk. When they realize how close Denver has been to capture, they may start answering questions hoping to make things easier for themselves."

Excited by their news, the couple hurried back to the shop. They joined Louise, Ken, and the Moffat sisters in the wax-making room. Jean and Chris reported what the captain had told them. Osmo stood in the open doorway and listened.

Winifred Moffat commented, "I'm glad those girls have been caught. I always said their mother was a troublemaker and they've inherited her mean disposition."

As she spoke, the doorbell rang and Osmo slipped away to answer it.

The Wax Queen smiled wanly from her bed. "I have had another ESP warning, but it is vague. The only thing that comes to me is an impression that I am in personal danger."

Jean questioned her gently, but she could not be more specific. Then the boys began to ask interested queries about ESP. The Queen told them about some of her experiences.

While they were talking, Louise noticed that the wax-room door, which had been standing open, was now closed. At first she assumed Osmo had done it, but the more Louise thought about it, the more she felt uneasy. She decided to investigate.

Louise crossed the room and tried to open the door. It was locked! Now fearful, she began to pound on it.

"What's the matter?" Mrs. Campbell asked.

Louise said calmly, "Someone has locked us in."

She had hardly finished speaking when a soft hissing noise came from underneath the door. At the same instant, she smelled a peculiar odor.

"Gas!" Louise exclaimed.

Alarmed, the boys looked around quickly. Ken pointed to the closed doors which led to the display room and the studio. "Can we get out through either of those?"

"Dead ends," replied Louise. "The rooms have no windows or doors. It would be only a matter of time before the gas filled them, too."

"Then we'll have to break this door down," Chris said. "Come on, Ken, we'll give it the old football rush."

As the boys stepped back and made ready, a man's hoarse voice came from the other side.

"It's too late! We're in charge now. You'll never make it! The place is filled with gas."

Angrily Jean cried out, "If that's true, how are you surviving it?"

"We have on gas masks."

Suddenly Louise thought about Osmo. "What have you done with the old man?" she asked in alarm.

There was a sardonic laugh from the other side of the door. "Don't worry about him. He'll soon be asleep."

"You can't get away with this," Louise said

desperately. The man who had spoken was not Moffat, but she was sure that the Queen's brother was in the shop.

"Fred, if you're out there, answer me," said the Wax Queen. "Let us out. I'll give you what you want."

The same man replied, "Moffat will get what he wants without your giving it to him. He says you had plenty of chances. Now it's too late."

"Your stepdaughters are in custody, Mr. Moffat," put in Jean. "They'll tell everything. You can't get away. Think what you're doing!"

The boys joined in the girls' pleas and arguments as the gas fumes grew stronger, but all their efforts brought no reply.

"Fred!" shouted Winnie Moffat. "Wendy will give you the shop and I'll provide you a steady income. If you don't care for your sisters, think of these young people!"

There was no response.

"It's no use," Miss Moffat said in a choking voice. "He's out there, that devil. But he won't speak to us."

"Fred, you must listen to reason," the Wax Queen called weakly. "Answer us."

There was a slight pause, then the man chortled and said, "The curse will not let any of you escape!"

CHAPTER XX

A Royal Discovery

"STAND back," Chris said to the Danas. "We're going to batter down that door."

He and Ken made a running start and hurled themselves against it.

"No use!" barked a man who had not spoken before. "There are two of us here with gas masks. We'll be more than a match for you!"

"That's Fred's voice," whispered the Wax Queen. "He's right. We're trapped!"

As she spoke, the gas fumes became stronger.

"There must be a way out!" exclaimed Louise as she muffled her nose with a handkerchief.

"The skylights!" said Jean. "Here and in the studio! If only we could reach those, we might open them and get air."

"They're rusted shut," said the Queen.

"Then we'll have to break this one," Chris said.

"It'll take two of us," remarked Ken. He looked around the room and decided to use the bed to stand on. "It's the only piece of furniture high enough to be of any use," he said.

The girls helped the Wax Queen to get up and sit in a chair.

Quietly the two boys carried the bed, now closed, to the center of the room and Ken jumped onto it. Chris climbed to his shoulders, reached up, and fumbled with the skylight. The others watched anxiously.

"Hurry," gasped Winnie Moffat, covering her face with a handkerchief.

Meanwhile, Jean hurried to the Queen's studio and returned with a sculpting tool and a cloth, which she passed up to Chris.

"Wait!" Louise called softly. "We don't want those men to hear you break the panes. They might increase the gas. Let's cause a commotion to cover the noise."

She drew Jean and the two women to the door, where they pounded and screamed to be let out, while Chris broke several panes of glass and caught the pieces in the cloth.

A wave of fresh air swept into the room.

"Oh," sighed the Wax Queen, "that's better!"

The boys leaped down quietly.

"One of us should go for the police," whispered Louise. "Do you think you could climb through the skylight, Chris?"

"I'll try," he said.

"The officers are staked out in the attic across

the street and there's one in a house behind this one," Jean told him.

Ken frowned. "Take it easy, Chris," he warned. "Those crooks might have a lookout stationed somewhere. If they spot you before you signal the police—" He left the sentence unfinished.

But the others knew only too well what he meant.

"Good luck," the Danas whispered as the boys once again climbed onto the chest. A minute later Chris had disappeared through the broken skylight.

The Wax Queen shivered. "It's getting chilly in here," she said, "and I'm worried about Osmo."

The group exchanged troubled glances. What had the men done with Osmo? Could he be lying unconscious in the gas-filled shop?

Louise did not want to frighten Mrs. Campbell more, but she realized that Osmo's life might depend upon how swiftly they made their escape.

"I think we'd better attempt to get out ourselves," Louise said quietly, "just in case Chris is stopped."

"But what can we do?" asked the Wax Queen.

"Pretend to be overcome," replied Ken. "Whoever is out there may look in to check on us. Then we'll rush him!"

"But suppose they just go away," said Jean. "We must do something to make them look in here."

Her sister agreed. "I know what! We'll pretend to be overcome, but make an odd noise." She picked up the metal sculpting tool, then hurried to the counter where the wax vats stood. One was empty. Louise signaled to Ken to carry it closer to the door. "I'll keep hitting this regularly," she whispered, "and I'll bet someone will open the door to see what's going on."

"Then we'll catch him and take his mask," said Ken. "I'm pretty sure I could barrel my way through those fellows."

At Louise's silent direction, the Moffat sisters withdrew to the center of the room. She, Jean, and Ken took up positions on either side of the door. Louise began a slow, insistent tapping on the metal vat.

In a few minutes someone pounded hard on the door. "Hey, what's going on in there?" called a gruff voice. No one answered and Louise kept tapping. A few moments later they heard the key turn in the lock. The door opened cautiously and a man in a gas mask stepped inside.

The next instant, Ken tackled him and threw the man to the floor. His head hit hard and he lay stunned. Swiftly Jean removed his mask and gave it to Ken, who put it on and dashed into the shop. There he came face to face with another masked man. Ken lunged and brought him down with a thud!

At the same moment, the shop door burst open and Chris entered with two plainclothesmen. They marched the prisoner into the big wax room, where one of the detectives hauled the second man to his feet. The Danas had recognized him as the burly one who followed them in the taxi and caused the near collision with the motorboat.

Meanwhile, the boys had turned off the gas which hissed from a large tank in the anteroom. One of the detectives was James Murphy. He stripped the mask from the thug Ken had tackled in the shop. Moffat!

"Where is Osmo?" Jean demanded.

"We locked him in the coat closet."

Jean and Louise ran to the anteroom and unlocked the closet. The old man was trembling, but unharmed. He had piled coats against the bottom of the door to keep out the gas fumes.

As the girls escorted him to the wax room, two policemen arrived with a lanky man held between them. Right behind was Captain Brown.

"We picked up this one sitting in a car around the corner," said the captain. He had the motor running and a gas mask on the seat beside him."

"This is the lot, then," said Detective Murphy, looking over the prisoners. "We saw two men get out of the car and enter the shop about half an hour ago," he told the Danas and their friends. "They were carrying two large cartons marked 'Wax,' so we thought nothing of it. We assumed they were helping the Wax Queen unpack them."

"The gas tank and masks were in those cartons," said Louise.

"You might as well confess," Captain Brown said to Moffat. "Your stepdaughters are in custody and have told us all about your campaign against the Wax Queen and your car-winning racket. You made a pretty profit selling each of those cars after you 'won' them, didn't you?"

Moffat glared, but said nothing.

Captain Brown turned to the Danas. "You were right in your theory about the Victoria bust. The girls said Moffat stole it both times. He planned to return it and exonerate his sister in exchange for the shop." The captain went on to confirm that the moving of the wax figure of Denver and the thefts of the other statues were done to frighten Mrs. Campbell into selling her shop to her brother.

"Where are those stolen busts?" Louise asked Moffat. Again the man did not reply.

The lanky prisoner threw a fearful glance at Moffat, but the burly accomplice spoke up. "I can tell you. They're in my apartment. I stole them and Moffat was going to sell them to a foreign wax museum." The man looked anxious. "My name is Ben Kroger. I was only Moffat's helper. Go easy on me and I'll talk."

"Where's the Victoria bust?" Louise asked, but Ben Kroger insisted he did not know. He confessed that he had gone to Mrs. Carson's apartment disguised in a beard to make a wax impression of the lock. "We were going to have a duplicate key made, then use it to get in and scare you off the case." Seeing Miss Dana leave, he had taken a chance that she had a key and seized her purse.

"Was it you, then, who got into the apartment house both times and knocked out the doorman?" Jean asked.

"That's right. I also wrote the lipstick messages and delivered the box to the restaurant, but Moffat made the trap himself. This other fellow here, Linky, snitched the key from the Queen's refrigerator and spied on you."

The tall man swallowed hard, then spoke up so indistinctly the girls could hardly understand him. "I only did what Fred told me to."

"What about the diamond?" Jean asked.

The accomplices looked blank and Moffat glanced up sharply.

Captain Brown said, "That surprises you, doesn't it, Moffat? You didn't know about the diamond." He explained that the man's stepdaughters had stolen it some weeks before but had not told Moffat. "Beth Bushwick said you often pried into their business, Moffat, and even went through their purses on the sly.

"Last Monday Beth had to go on an errand. Her sister was out at the time, and Beth was afraid that while both of them were gone, you would discover the diamond. So she made a hole in the black wax cat, inserted the jewel, and hid the figure in a drawer. While she was gone, Dora came home and you ordered her to go to the shop to spot the Nefertiti statue, which you intended her to spray later with sulfur dioxide. Thinking the cat would make a good excuse to go to the shop, Dora searched and found it. She deliberately chipped the figure, then took it in for repair. She neglected to mention this to Beth, who did not notice it was gone until this morning. When Beth told her sister what was in it, Dora hastened to get the cat back, and while at the shop, sprayed the statue with the chemical."

Moffat's face was like a thundercloud. "Those girls have been nothing but trouble to me! Always complaining that they didn't get a fair share of the car proceeds! In fact, the night of the Penfield carnival, they tried to run away in the prize car and I had to chase them. I thought I'd managed to talk sense into them after that, but I guess I didn't."

"You must have had some trick which enabled your stepdaughters to choose the winning number every time," said Louise. "What was it?"

Captain Brown spoke up. "The girls told us that. There was a small staple in the winning ticket and a magnet in the ring the girl wore. When she put her hand in the barrel and swished it around, the stapled ticket clung to the ring."

"What I don't understand," Winnie Moffat

said to her brother, "is why you wanted Wendy's shop."

Moffat sneered. "I intended to make some real money with it. First I'd have sold the valuable antiques. Then I'd have hired a cheap artist to make copies of all Wendy's pieces and sell them as originals. There's no telling how long I could've gone on raking in the money."

"What did you hope to accomplish by gassing these people?" asked Detective Murphy.

Moffat looked balefully at the Danas. "For one thing, revenge on the Danas. They queered my car racket. When my spy reported they had gone to Oak Falls, I didn't dare go through with the drawing there. Later I got a tip that the police were on to me at Harper. I knew it was their doing."

"And to get even with us you would make everyone else suffer?" asked Louise.

Moffat shrugged. "With my twin sisters out of the way, I wouldn't have Winnie hounding me and I could get my hands on the shop."

"You've a lot to answer for, Moffat," remarked Captain Brown. "I wouldn't like to be in your shoes."

"Please, Fred," said the Wax Queen, "tell us where the Victoria bust is."

Her brother smiled unpleasantly. "No, I won't. You and Winnie were never fair to me, and now I'm in a lot of trouble because you put these Danas on my trail. I'm doing nothing for you!"

"Your trouble is your own fault," Louise pointed out sternly.

"Fred," the Wax Queen said earnestly, "the law must take its course, but I will forgive all you've done and even help you get a good lawyer if you will tell where the Victoria bust is. It is a real treasure. We must get it back unharmed."

Moffat started to say No, then stopped, and a bright glint came into his hard black eyes. "Sure, I'll tell you," he said smoothly and paused. He looked around at the expectant faces. Suddenly he laughed. "Poor Wendy. Everybody walks all over the Wax Queen."

Puzzled, the listeners waited for him to say more. But he only rocked on his heels and smirked.

"Come on," Captain Brown said sharply, and the police took the prisoners away.

"I wonder what he means," the Wax Queen said unhappily. "I don't think anyone has taken advantage of me—except him."

Her sister sighed. "You know Fred. He was always cantankerous. He never meant to tell us where it was."

Suddenly an idea came to Louise. "Wait a minute," she said slowly. "Maybe he *did* tell us."

"What do you mean?" Ken asked as the others looked surprised.

Then Jean gave a little gasp. "Of course!" she exclaimed. "He's tricky and it would be just like him to tell us in such a way that we wouldn't realize he had done so. He'd think it was a great joke on us."

"I get it!" exclaimed Chris. "That's a terrific idea!"

" 'Everybody walks all over the Wax Queen,' " Louise repeated. "It must mean she's below us somewhere. Is there a cellar?"

"Yes," Mrs. Campbell said quickly. "Osmo— show them."

The man led the way out of the shop and opened the street door leading to the apartment. At the foot of the stairs, Osmo pulled aside a small rug, revealing a trap door. Ken seized the ring in it and pulled up the door.

"Take my pencil flashlight," said Chris as the Danas started down a ladder into the darkness below. Before long, the thin beam caught the sparkle of a jeweled crown and swept over the pale, serious face of the wax Victoria.

A few minutes later the girls placed the treasure carefully on the workstand in the Queen's studio, while the boys watched proudly and Winnie Moffat heaved a great sigh of relief.

The Danas did too. The case was solved! But in a short time they were to find themselves involved in another mystery, *The Secret of the Minstrel's Guitar.*

Mrs. Campbell drew near Victoria and gently

touched the statue. She smiled with tears in her eyes. "I am so glad to see it safe. Now we can return the statue. You Danas have been wonderful!"

Louise laughed and said, "It's nice to have the two Wax Queens, face to face!"

Jean gave the sculptress an affectionate squeeze. "And I am glad that this one is smiling now!"